WHAT THE CRITICS SAY:

"Like many novels for and by women, strikingly intelligent and tough-minded."
—*New York Times Book Review*

"This is an excellent novel, one difficult to put down once you are well into the story."
—*Library Journal*

"The denouement is profound and unexpected. There was no way Ivor could overcome his impotence. In this presentation the author makes a strong appeal to our capacity for charity and compassion."
—*Best Sellers*

A CASE
IN NULLITY

by

Evelyn Berckman

Belmont Books • New York City

A CASE IN NULLITY

A BELMONT BOOK—December 1971

Published by

Belmont Productions, Inc.
185 Madison Avenue
New York, New York 10016

Copyright © MCMLXVII by Evelyn Berckman

Library of Congress Catalog Card Number 68-11768

Printed in the United States of America.

Published by special arrangement with Doubleday & Company, Inc.

ABOUT THE AUTHOR

Evelyn Berckman, born in Philadelphia, has lived in London since 1960. Her career has been a varied one. For many years she was a pianist and a composer whose works have been performed by the Philadelphia Orchestra and the Pro Arte Quartet. She has written plays and nonfiction in addition to her novels (which include *The Heir of Starvelings* and *She Asked For It*) and is at work on an historical study, *The Hidden Navy*.

For
Clyde Marshall-Reynolds, Q.C.,
Bencher of the Middle Temple
Special Divorce Commissioner
With thanks and love.

A nullity: English legal term for a divorce-suit
based on the grounds of non-consummation of
a marriage.

1

When Auriol Hailes left her husband, the realization that she had left a lunatic did not relieve her. It only frightened her, and it frightened her because her husband's lunacy was of a special kind. He was intelligent and amusing; his judgment was usually right, if too malicious and merciless; he had accomplished manners, he was well read and widely travelled, and had expertise enough to have made a collection of watches and snuff-boxes, small but of concentrated beauty and value. Clever about money, he had private resources, and also an interest in a stockbroking firm that gave him a maximum return for a minimum of time and attention.

His lunacy, in a word, was invisible, having to do with one area only in his physical, mental, and spiritual makeup—the area of sex. Or more accurately, sexual affront; this was the single malign element that, with baleful chemistry, changed him from Ivor Hailes into someone completely unrecognizable. Since only a closest intimate could be aware of this hidden coil, and since even on his wife its dimensions had dawned gradually, it found her, in last resorts, the sole person aware of the state of affairs; all the more alone since he was not in the habit of intimate friendships nor, indeed, of intimacy of any sort.

Her meditations and conclusions about this

knowledge—in the intervals of planning her next step—took place in the drab semi-service flat on the shabbier fringes of South Ken where she had gone to ground. Perpetually, if obscurely, it troubled her that this old house with its thick walls and solid doors gave her no feeling of refuge. She had only fled, not escaped. She was not such a fool as to think she could escape the aftermath of Ivor Hailes by a mere change of address or a shifting of the place where she put her feet or her chair or her bed. Too profoundly, in her inmost fibre, she felt the damage of her association with him, the broken places no longer deepening but not yet closing. As for the house she had left, the little house in the charming mews, the delicious little house stuffed full of lovely things—and of Ivor Hailes's emanations—she had not even the shadow of a regret, or more precisely she tried not to think of it, ever. Its gloss and opulence had taken on for her a sinister quality, the life-withering horror of a desert; by comparison, the neutral shabbiness of the place where she now lived had about it something soothing, even homelike.

From this mediocre setting, her marriage, when she looked back over it—and she had plenty of time for backward looks—seemed to separate itself into three distinct compartments: the drugged period, the nightmare, and the waking.

2

At this horrible party, and other parties exactly similar, she had one job: to circulate. That people should stand alone on the outskirts of the crowded din, obviously without acquaintance or anyone to talk to, was frowned upon by her employers; such oases of isolation must be spotted, taken in tow, brayed into the general mass. This was Auriol Chapman's function, to revolve ceaselessly and see that no one was left out. And conscientiously she revolved, moving from group to group, introducing newcomers, pressing drinks and appetizers on this one and that, greeting and rallying people on a changeless accent of gaiety and laughter—the charming young woman with russet hair showing under the big fashionable hat, the lovely figure and quick graceful movements, and the lightless, hopeless void of death in her heart, the unceasing pain.

In the two immense white-and-gold rooms, very lofty and brilliantly lighted, packed solid with people, conversational uproar and bright fog of cigarette smoke, her patrol brought her to one enlivening haven; the corner where stood Maggie Bolter, knocking back her fourth or fifth martini (this early) and regarding the assembly with the air of enigmatic scorn, unconcealed, that was one of her specialties; Maggie with her foghorn voice, her shattering vocabulary, and her intelligence

11

like a welding torch, with the same white-hot blaze and overspill of ideas. Now, once again in the course of her rounds, Auriol reached the short heavy woman, unprepossessing in tweeds that gave her almost an oblong shape, and received the impact of her deepening scowl and uninhibited voice.

"For Christ's sake, shindies like this," Maggie trumpeted. "Ushering into the world another rotten book, three hundred and sixty-four pages of smart bright nothing at all. What do publishers expect of these grisly covens—that by magic they'll change muck into something good?"

"That's right," Auriol approved warmly. "A little louder, can't you, so the author won't miss it? He's standing not ten feet away from you."

"In this abattoir," Maggie bellowed, "it could be ten miles—he can't hear us. We can hardly hear each other, if it comes to that."

True enough; Auriol shrugged and moved off again on the treadmill of hospitality, and yet for a second with only her body on it, not her mind. Knowing Maggie as long as she had, with an affection that was old, constant, and curiously important to her, it was yet a considerable tribute to Maggie's quality that any contact with her, however fleeting, could still magnetize attention, and rivet speculation upon herself. And now on Auriol's mind, with all the mind's power of simultaneous imagery, there focussed itself that familiar, yet compelling, rabble of diversities that were the portrait of Maggie. Of all the people Auriol had ever met, professionally or otherwise, no one could touch her in ruthless evaluation of talent, a gift which had enabled her to make a comfortable lot of money out of her actors' agency, even after taxes. Her power of estimating character was similarly ferocious, except that this was only part of it; she had a faculty, almost alarming, of divining the secret springs that set a person in motion, and this faculty, overpassing mere acuteness of judgment, extended into the uncharted, impalpable areas of clairvoyance. Au-

riol, while regarding her as given to savage prejudices, had never known her radically wrong on any
point of real importance—or so seldom that she never
any more, though once she had, attempted to dispute
her decisions. Aside from this savagery, which she reserved for the spurious, pretentious, or unkind, Maggie
was a mere defenceless jelly of compassion, perfectly
incapable of seeing misery and not going to the rescue.
That ingratitude was usually her return made no difference; about gratitude she was realistic and sceptical,
and derived most of her solace—apparently—from
being the slave of the worst-spoiled bevy of dogs ever
gathered under one roof, and for whose exclusive
benefit she maintained a country cottage . . .

Auriol's attention, suddenly absenting itself from
Maggie, returned and clamped itself on present circumstance. She had seen that forbidden quantity, a solitary
being on the fringes of the scrum and making no attempt to penetrate to its inner parts; a very young man,
standing alone. He had the air of a stranger there, and
certainly she had never see him before. At once she
began making her way toward him with professional so-
licitude, ready, with her hostess's mortar and pestle, to
blend him into the general coagulation.

When she got through the haze of cigarette smoke
and nearer to him, she found that her impression of him
had been misleading. He was older than she had
thought; the appearance of youth that he conveyed, at a
distance, was due to his slenderness and strikingly lithe
carriage. He had a clear pale skin and strongly arched
eyebrows above eyes very dark brown or black. His
chin was firm, the mouth saved from being too shapely
by the thinness of the lips; his nose, not finely chiseled
but straight, had a very slight concavity just between the
eyes. This harmonized with the flatness of his cheeks
and gave him a note of attractiveness slightly exotic. It
was a face much more distinct than the general run of
faces, additionally set off by the elegance of its owner.
For he was elegant, surpassingly so, now that she was

13

near enough to see the nuances of his tailoring. By and large she would place him in the middle thirties, eight or ten years older than she had thought on seeing him from across the room.

"Good day!" she said loudly against the uproar, and offered her hand. "I'm Auriol Chapman."

"Good day," he answered—presumably; not having raised his voice, he was almost inaudible. "I'm . . . "

"Sorry," she apologized. "I didn't quite . . . ? Excuse me for yelling," she added, with automatic sprightliness.

"This infernal din," he said more loudly.

"I know. But it means a good party, doesn't it?" She laughed her professional laugh. "The more noise the more successful, I expect." If she could somehow pick up the threads that connected him with this gathering, she would be able to steer him to the people he wanted to meet; as it was, she had not even got his name. "Are you a writer?"

"God forbid." He had raised his voice, but only just; his air of making an isolated effort, which he was not disposed to repeat, was discouraging.

"I see. Well, is there—"

"Oh Lord, this is hopeless." He had interrupted all at once, casting about the assembly a glance of comprehensive contempt. Before she realized, he had taken her wrist with a sort of light authority perfectly unexpected but not unpleasant, and led her through a door. Just beyond it he stopped, turning to face her. "There," he said. "That's better."

It was; the hall was long and quite empty except for a man at the far end, shepherding coats and hats. By contrast with the packed room the air seemed almost fresh, the tiled floor gave off a coolness, and they were able to talk in normal voices.

"I'm Ivor Hailes," he went on. "And you're Mrs. Chapman, you said—?"

"Miss."

"Sorry, I didn't hear." When he smiled, only one corner of his mouth moved; she could not decide whether or not she liked the effect. "You were circulating for dear life in there, weren't you?"

"I'd better," she returned. "It's my job to circulate."

"Is it? what's your connection with this flea market?"

"I'm with Stormonth," she explained. "I'm an editor."

"Dear me." He was respectful but faintly mocking. "Don't you get bored with the twaddle they call fiction?"

"I'm not a fiction editor," she explained. "Just history and biography."

"I stand rebuked."

"Don't," she adjured, lamely enough. "I'm not marked with it on my forehead, or anything."

"So you're a historical and biographical editor," he pursued, with that same blend of slight mockery and burlesque awe. "That means, doesn't it, that you could teach history if you liked?"

"Yes, I could." She shuddered. "But I'd die first. Teach? the mere thought of it withers me."

"Let's not think of it then—we mustn't wither you." Still he continued surveying her with the same half-smiling look, enigmatic but curiously intent, except that now their colloquy was beginning to make her impatient. If only he would drop some hint as to his connection with this party, she could steer him toward the proper person or group . . .

"So you consider yourself better off where you are? you're satisfied and happy with your life?" he continued his amiable inquisition. Obviously he was ready to pursue a leisurely conversation as if the two of them were alone in a private room, instead of this crowded place where a dozen responsibilities pressed on her; the realization annoyed her actively enough to make her break off their exchanges abruptly and decisively, and take charge.

"Mr. Hailes." She reassumed her mantle of professional briskness. "Let me find you a drink and something to eat—"

"No, thank you," he interrupted with equal decision. "Nothing to eat and nothing to drink. Not here, at least."

"Then come with me," she invited, anxious to get back. "You must meet some people."

"Must I?" he murmured. "I'm quite happy here, you know."

"Well, but . . ." momentarily at a loss, she rallied. "You came here to meet someone, didn't you? Everyone does."

"I'm not everyone," he informed her coolly. "I came with a friend." His manner somehow barred her from asking the identity of this friend. "Against my better judgment—publishers' parties are all alike. Tell me," he digressed all at once, looking through the door. In his glance, his voice, was something new—a concentration, an alertness? She could not, this quickly, define it.

"—tell me," he was saying. "Who's that type over there—with the shoulders?"

"That?" Her gaze followed his. "That's one of ours too—Tom M'Kell."

"With Stormonth also, you mean? Is he your boss?"

"Oh, no," she disclaimed. "I've nothing to do with him, directly. He's with the art department. Head of it, actually."

"Art," he murmured. By some management of nuance he made the words not only disparagement, but condemnation; his eyes were still riveted to M'Kell. "Well meaning, isn't he?"

"Why . . . " She was astounded, also completely at sea. "He—he's very nice."

"I'm sure of it," agreed Hailes. "Loyal, wouldn't he be?"

From mere bewilderment she was silent; he was continuing, "And decent, and jolly, one can tell it to look at him.—Oh Lord," he interpolated suddenly. "He's seen us—he's coming this way. He would, wouldn't he?"

Her back was squarely to the doorway, nor did she turn; obscurely troubled, transfixed, she could plot

Tom's approach by the impression in the other man's eyes. It was the back of her neck, accordingly, that received Tom's jovial blast of, "Skulking, Roly? skulkig?" He had opened all the stops on the stentorian voice that did him such good service on occasions like these; as she looked around, he stood beaming at them in all the impressiveness of his six feet and proportionate build, the ingenuous warmth of his nice blunt features, the disorder of his dark-blond hair, always laboriously flattened for such functions and always standing up in spikes at the end.

"Is this an ambush?" he demanded, his eyes touching on the male half of the colloquy. "Roly, I don't think I've met—"

"Mr. Hailes," she said hastily, "this is Mr. M'Kell."

"How d'you do," said Tom, and thrust out a big hand, and Hailes extended his own. His manner of doing it, for all its understatement, conveyed the unwilling fastidiousness of one forced to touch something unpleasant. This was so overt that it checked even the Niagara of Tom's geniality. A curious silence fell for the fraction of a second; both men looked at each other.

"You've no drink," said Tom, recovering. "Roly, you're not looking after Mr. Hailes properly."

"Miss Chapman has been looking after me admirably," Hailes put in. His thinly pinched voice matched his thinly pinched lips, which barely moved in speaking. "Don't trouble yourself on my account, I beg."

"Well then—" Tom faltered slightly, again disconcerted, but too puzzled—obviously—to be offended. Auriol looked on with discomfort; it was painful to see the friendly St. Bernard rebuffed. "—see you," he was saying. "Happy to've . . ." He moved off.

"*What* did he call you?" Hailes demanded at once, with knit brows. He had asked it so quickly as to amputate her own instant attempt to speak. "Roly?"

"Mr. Hailes," she said coldly, ignoring the question. She felt an active animosity toward him on Tom's account—and on her own, for having been obliged to witness the episode. "I must be returning to the fray. It's been pleasant to—"

"You're angry with me," he accused indulgently; his lips quirked with amusement. "Aren't you?"

"No," she said stiffly, and for an instant let her anger be seen. Yet, for all this hostility, she was a little taken aback. "Good-bye."

"Please don't go," he besought, and to her moment of disconcertment was added surprise. Nevertheless—

"Sorry," she murmured, yet without the steely edge of a moment ago. "Afraid I must. Good-bye," she repeated, turning about and re-entering the room; it was not until his voice was close in her ear that she realized he had followed her.

"I behaved badly," he admitted. "And for a punishment, you're leaving me."

From sheer unpreparedness, and barely past the threshold, she stopped in her tracks.

"Please," he cajoled, and circled around into her line of vision. "Don't punish me."

"I—I'm not," she stammered, her anger dissipated against her own will. "But actually I must go, I'm not here just for ornament, you know."

"Three minutes," he bargained. "Stop with me for three minutes. The party won't disintegrate without you that soon, will it?"

Unwilling yet half-smiling, she hesitated; he seized on the barely perceptible pause with the promptness of a military tactician. "I was watching you, before," he said. "Whirling and darting about. I was hoping you'd get to me, you know, and talk to me."

"W-were you?" she stammered again, foolishly. The unforeseen turn of the conversation was not only disarming her to the point of limpness, but depriving her of even the commonest currencies of speech.

"And if you hadn't got to me," he pursued equably, "I was coming after you. And you're still annoyed with me." He smiled, patently amused. "Because of that tame mastodon of yours. Well, never mind."

18

Her annoyance flared again, but not quickly enough; while she still groped for a devastating retort to his dismissiveness, he had added, "I've decided that you work too hard."

"I don't," she rebuffed ineffectually. "I don't at all."

"Much too hard," he pursued calmly, as if she had not spoken. "You look tired."

"I'm not in the least tired," she snapped, while a silent voice in her concurred, *Yes, I'm deathly tired, I've had nothing but tiredness and death in me for a year and a half, but I won't say so to you, you stranger.*

"You need a bit of distraction," he went on, ignoring her, but his manner of doing it was somehow a caress. "Have dinner with me this evening."

Again her surprise at the invitation—totally unexpected—capped her indecision with additional speechlessness.

"If you're free," he was continuing. "Are you?"

"Well—well, I am," she faltered. "But this—"

"Lord, yes." He had not needed her gesture toward the party. "This shambles'll go on and on, of course. But later, when it's over? Say nine-thirty, or ten?"

"I expect I could." Her acceptance was halting. "Thank you very much."

"Ten, let's say? Be on the safe side?" He smiled at her. "The Mirabelle?"

"I shan't have time to dress," she warned him.

He laughed aloud, and subconsciously she registered that his laugh, like his speaking voice, was charming.

"You're lovely," he assured her, and with one fingertip stroked her sapphire-mink stole. "Opulently lovely."

"Opulently," she returned. "It's rented."

He laughed again with apparent delight and—she noted, with puzzlement—on an odd note of satisfaction.

"Ten o'clock," he repeated. "The Mirabelle."

She nodded and smiled, moving away, yet was aware that his own movement to be off was checked by an unknown man's coming up and engaging him in conversation; it looked like something from which he would not escape in a hurry, and rather maliciously she was glad to see him trapped, after his lofty dismissal of the room and everyone in it. Then once more she was putting her shoulders to the festive wheel—running down, however—whose slower and slower revolutions brought her in due course to Maggie's corner and to Maggie's inexhaustible cornucopia of benevolent sentiments.

"Wassail," she bellowed. "Boys and girls together, or the cannibal's love-feast. Half the fakes in this room're ready to cut the other half's throats, and what loss if they did? I ask you." From an ambulant tray she snatched a fresh martini; what number in the series, Auriol declined even to guess.

"Eat something, why don't you?" she hazarded.

"Eat this muck?" Dramatically Maggie recoiled from the offering of a passing waiter. "Take it away, man, don't shove your worms of piped cream cheese and anchovies under *my* nose. Nor," her objurgation pursued his hasty retreat, "your clammy toast stuck with dead red leather, miscalled smoked salmon."

"Some day, at one of these things," predicted Auriol, "there'll be a sudden lull and you in the middle, loud and clear." She prepared to resume her wanderings, well aware that Maggie was one of those hard drinkers no longer capable of getting really drunk.

"The moment of truth," returned Maggie, and took a hasty swig. "When all this stink's died down, have dinner with me."

"Oh Maggie, why didn't you ask me before?" Auriol always felt a sort of guilt at having to refuse any invitation of this lonely woman's. "I'm so sorry."

"You're eating with Do or Nora? Couldn't the three of us—?"

"Not with them," Auriol admitted. Her constraint and reluctance must look offensively like coyness, she thought, under the regard of two small and sharp grey eyes, and felt somehow compelled to explain, even to excuse herself, though surely there was occasion for neither. "A man."

"Well," Maggie said, after a moment. Never one to dissimulate her emotions, she was glum with discontent and disappointment.

"I'm sorry," Auriol apologized again.

"Well," Maggie repeated, and shrugged. "Next time." Out of her overcast of sulkiness, a small spark of curiosity showed itself for an instant. "Who is he? someone here?"

Auriol looked around cautiously, and was surprised to see her escort of the evening still pinioned in talk upon the same spot, and by the same unknown man.

"Just beside the door," she murmured. "That's he—the dark man talking to the tall blond one."

Maggie's glance, with wavering focus, followed the direction of Auriol's, and with visible effort finally isolated its objective. The instant after, in her alarming and disconcerting way, she seemed to have accomplished the transition from muzzy to cold sober.

"Him?" she said blankly. "You're having dinner with *him*?"

"Yes." The fact of Maggie's inflection was unmistakable, if not its meaning. "Why, do you know him?"

"Never saw him before in my life," the other shrugged. To her sullen look was added an aloofness.

"But you—you sound as if you knew him," persisted Auriol, considerably puzzled. "Why, is there anything about him that—"

"Nothing!" Maggie interrupted temperishly. "I told you, I don't know him from a rented suit at Moss Brothers. Better shove off on your errands of mercy, hadn't you, Little Sister of Dolorous Canapés?—Hoi! you!" Like lightning she had ravished a martini from a passing waiter. "Good night, mate. Enjoy yourself." Without moving, she had seemed to withdraw into measureless and forbidding distance.

Auriol shrugged in turn and passed on, carrying away from the episode not only bafflement but a faint worry —quickly rubbed away, however, by the erosion of succeeding encounters and talk. It was an old tale that

Maggie specialized in prejudices and dislikes as sudden as they were virulent, and her ordinary conversational style was of such a nature as to make it a constant wonder that—considering the peculiar alertness and vitality of libel law in her native land—she had so far escaped with a whole skin. This was merely another of Maggie's jagged excursions, Auriol dismissed the matter —until another aspect of the encounter was revived by Tom, accosting her with obvious purpose.

"Who's your boy friend," he demanded, towering over her, "that you were being clandestine with in the hall?"

"I don't know, except his name," she returned. "Ivor Hailes. It's the first time I'd met him."

"Me too, far as I know. So what," demanded Tom, "could he have against me? you noticed—?"

Auriol nodded.

"You couldn't very well not," he concurred. "And I swear I've never seen him before, yet there's no question he's got his knife into me, for some reason." He frowned. "Peculiar bloke."

Silent, she felt an agreement and a faint misgiving, as at some danger signal remotely heard.

"How'd he get here?" Tom was pursuing. "Who brought him?"

"A friend, he said. He didn't enlarge on it," Auriol explained, "and I didn't ask. Anyway, I'd no time."

"Well—" Tom shrugged, and punished his hair into a final dishevelment. Then he was washed away on a tidal stream of late-comers, leaving in Auriol a renewed, vague unease. Also, revolving punctiliously once more, she noted that Maggie's corner was now empty of Maggie, and felt somehow abandoned.

Well after nine, as Hailes had predicted, she was free at last, duty fulfilled down to the last crumb, the obligation of huddling with her colleagues at Stormonth for last comments, comparisons, and rehashing. Hurrying down the hall whose cold unpeopled silence was in itself a release, her passing glance at a mirror brought her up short all at once, almost startled; it showed her a face so much more alive than she had seen it for months. Then she emerged from the old house—once magnificent and now faintly seedy, maintained and rented out for functions like the one just over—and stepped out to the portico and the vision of Belgrave Square on a damp wretched evening. Upon the clammy insistent wind came the carbolic smell of coal fires burning somewhere, a London smell; lines of rain glistened momentarily as they threaded through the indeterminate light of street lamps; the pavements shone greasy and treacherous. It was the moment of let-down after the party, when the solitary being is returned to his solitude. But the moment had no power over her, for this one evening. She was glad, glad that instead of dining with Maggie, or going back to her solitary flat and some late scrambled eggs when fatigue would let her get around to them, a man was waiting for her—an attractive man and a charming restaurant and a dinner of the utmost accomplishment. Her heart rose with pleasure, then fell leaden with grief and shame and apology, then in spite of herself struggled upward again. It was her first real date since the death of the man she had been going to marry, seventeen months ago.

Undressing at one in the morning she had another awakening, sudden, to the fact of her own appearance. With a stocking halfway down her leg, with a surprise almost stupid, she sat before her mirror and stared at the still-lingering souvenirs of the evening's exhilaration: the delicate apricot flush in her cheeks, her half-smiling lips and brilliant eyes, amber rather than brown, with short dark-gold lashes. Her hair was an exquisite shade, not golden but of a muted fawn colour; her skin was of a fairness to go with this tan hair, not with blond. These felicities had been her offering to Giles, and at the thought of him, her mouth suddenly ugly with grief and her heart withering, she whimpered aloud, "Oh Christ, Oh Giles, Giles." The formula, the stale, idiotic formula: night, slippery roads, the sharp turn, the nobody in his car going nowhere in particular and having to do it at eighty miles an hour—and Giles, the universe that was Giles, destroyed; wiped out, and all for nothing . . .

But at once she tried to drive away the thought, then realized, startled, that this was the first time since his death that she had found it in herself to essay even a hint of resistance; for seventeen months, dragged at by memory and despair, she had not struggled against the leaden weight but let it, willingly, pull her deeper and deeper down. *I'm twenty-seven,* she pressed on, reasoning herself into this first renewal of living. *I may have fifty years ahead of me, or worse. Somehow I've got to go on.* But a feeling of betrayal so drowned her that she had, literally, to struggle for breath, like a determined but weakening swimmer through lethal currents. *Some day I'd have had to pick myself up and go on,* the argument with herself continued. *I always knew I'd have to, one day,* but she felt no conviction. And yet, strangely, it was not unpleasant to think that perhaps the day had come; not unpleasant to feel the pulsation of interest and hope, after the vacuum of grief; not unpleasant to see her beauty becoming authentic again instead of half-valid, cancelled for so long beneath her lost and haunted look. Actually (she had to admit) she had had with her new acquaintance a good evening, distinctly gay; they had found no end of things to talk about and had amused each other very well.

Giles, she entreated silently, needing to be forgiven for her pleasant evening. *I'll never meet anyone like you again,* she told him, and she was quite right, she never did.

This first step in her acquaintance with Ivor Hailes had no essential difference from the other steps that led her to a registry office one morning in August, five months later, when she ceased to be Auriol Chapman and became Auriol Hailes.

3

Now her mother need worry about her no longer.

It was a curious first thought for a honeymoon, yet she was less present in the car that drove them away from the registry than in the small flat in Paddington, the two rooms made pleasant through Auriol's hard-hitting attack on its original gloom and inconvenience and her continuing attention to its embellishment, since Mrs. Chapman's health permitted her to do little for her surroundings. She was naturally very gentle, timid and unworldly (she and her husband had been an unworldly couple, he a valuer of books for an august firm of auctioneers), and gave in too much to an undoubted heart condition, allowing it to drain her of what little energy she possessed. Worse, she seemed to shrink perpetually beneath some impending, shapeless calamity; the shock of her husband's death, then the disaster that had overtaken her fixed income, had dealt the final blow to her sense of security and stock of confidence. When confronted by Auriol's misfortune, the sudden death of her fiancé, she was first of all crushed beneath the knowledge of her uselessness as a prop or support to her daughter; since then she had lost ground so visibly that any stress or apprehension could be seen, also visibly, to loosen her hold on life. And of this fragile state, a new manifestation was her sad disposition to be alone and of preferring to be alone. There was another weight on Auriol's heart; her defenceless mother had always evoked from her that anxious love so cruelly touched with pain, and latterly this love had become fiercely, furiously protective.

"I'm going to be married, Mummy."

"Oh darling!" Such joy had begun to illumine Mrs. Chapman at once that it made her frailness almost incandescent. "Oh, darling, I'm glad, I'm so *glad!*"

"I'm glad you're glad." Auriol laughed foolishly, on a half-sob; the same note had been in her mother's voice.

"Oh yes, yes, dearest, I . . . I mean, one can't spend one's whole life in the past, can one, I mean—"

Too sharply, Auriol interrupted. "Well, it's nice that you approve."

"Approve! Oh, it's marvelous." Tears were in Mrs. Chapman's eyes, eyes which Auriol remembered as charmingly bright and pretty; bereavement and illness had put paid to that. "Oh, my love, I hope you'll be happy, I hope you'll be so, so happy."

The word, repeated, aroused in Auriol a sort of flinching, as at an accusation not formulated; evading it, she asked indulgently, "Don't you want to know who he is? or anything about him?"

"Oh—why—of course, darling." Mrs. Chapman's acquiescence was hurried and a bit guilty, as if her memory had been suddenly jogged about some trifle. "Of course I do. Tell me."

"Well, his name's Ivor Hailes and he's thirty-six and he's quite nice-looking, interesting-looking—Oh well, I needn't describe him, you'll be meeting him. He's—ah —I think he's well-off—more than well-off, actually."

"That's always nice, darling," said Mrs. Chapman in the unmistakable accent of inattention.

"He has the most beautiful little house in Ellesmere Mews, perfect, just like a jewel. He'll get something bigger, he says but there's no hurry." She checked an instant, wondering why she said *He'll get* instead of *We'll*

26

get; the plural habit was new to her, she excused herself, and fled from the memory that with Giles she had always thought, naturally as breathing, in terms of *we*. "He collects things, watches and so forth, he's got marvelous taste. And he's clever and amusing—very nice to be with."

"That's nice, darling," repeated Mrs. Chapman on exactly the same placid, absent-minded note.

"And he—he has an office, I believe—" she stopped suddenly. How little she knew about him, in fact; only now, having to tell of him, she realized his degree of reticence, his annoying secretiveness about the most ordinary things, such as come out among ordinary people in the course of day-to-day exchanges. "—he must be a partner, or I expect so, they're stockbrokers. And he has very strong likes and dislikes, unexpected—I mean his mind works unexpectedly. That doesn't mean he isn't perfectly agreeable, for he is. I mean—" She stopped again, hearing how laboured she sounded, almost apologetic, and wondering why. But of all this, apparently, her mother remained oblivious.

"He sounds very nice," Mrs. Chapman murmured. "I'm sure I shall be tremendously fond of him." Her gaze, distant, scanned the radiant perspectives of Auriol's being married; in her state of beatitude, she was immune to other considerations. "Anyone you loved—"

"I've given up my job," Auriol digressed. The words, no less than the thought, gave her a panicky feeling of having relinquished some last handhold; of falling through space. But her mother's peaceful "Oh?" demonstrated that the sense of disaster was confined to herself alone. "You have, my dear?"

"Yes. Ivor—I mean—he disliked the idea of my keeping it. And I mean, my being away from ten to four-thirty, five days in the week, well, I could see how he . . ."

"Indeed yes." Mrs. Chapman's vagueness did not extend to her ideas on love and marriage. "He was quite right. A girl marrying a man that's well-to-do, why should she work in an office day after day? It's not sensible. Yes, he was right, and you were right to do as he wished. It's the beginning of your married life," she pointed out. "You couldn't start by disregarding his wishes straightaway. You couldn't begin your lives together with a serious difference of opinion."

"No," mumbled Auriol. Disconsolate, she felt that something was unsaid, but failed to discover what. "And we're going to have a quiet wedding," she added, for some reason hastily. "We'll go to a registry office, we're neither of us church-goers and there's no reason to—"

An unbidden picture splintered her mind for one instant, a cottage print of exaggerated verdure and flowers spangled with sunshine, an idealized rural felicity. Giles had wanted them to be married in the Staffordshire country church near his parents' home, and though its bells were flat-toned and jangly he was going to have the verger and two helpers ring a peal.

"Mummy," she pressed on inconsequently, "I'm going to get you a really good television set, you might even have it tomorrow."

"Oh, lovely." In Mrs. Chapman's delicate face was the glow, translucent, of genuine pleasure. "What a lovely present from both of you. Mr. Hailes—Ivor—must have a splendid one, I expect."

"Oh, no," Auriol returned. "He loathes them."

Her second honeymoon thought was also incongruous. First her mother: now Maggie. The only two people dug deep in her affections—outside of Ivor, she reminded herself hastily—yet their two images side by side made her smile at their sheer incongruity. Her mother, a pattern in dry faded lace, and foul-mouthed, swashbuckling Maggie . . . the picture disappeared, tinged by a last, fleeting thought: whether it were a mistake to have brought Maggie and Ivor together at all, for she had introduced them at a fairly early stage of the proceedings.

Ivor's first honeymoon utterance, not less out of drawing than his wife's first honeymoon thought, was sufficiently a duplication of her own to startle her. He and she often echoed each other in this way, and often at the same moment; she had taken it as an indication of their unison of spirit. In any case, this was the precise moment he chose to say, "That friend of yours, that thundering female—?"

"Maggie?" she returned. "Maggie Bolter?"

"Ghastly name. Ghastly woman," he observed, always affable. "How d'you put up with her?"

"You don't know her." Auriol took up the cudgels ineptly; his condemnations always seemed to weaken her to the point of ineffectualness. "I grant you she's a bit startling."

"Startling?" he echoed gently, and took his eyes from his driving long enough to give her an enigmatic glance. "Is that what you call it?"

"She's pure gold." Stoutly his wife strove against the undivined reticences of his tone. "And a tremendous friend."

"Ah," he murmured, and darted her another look, complex with indulgence and mocking challenge, as if he accused her of misunderstanding him wilfully. Aloud, all he said was, "People impose on you." Did his inflection say, *Now that I'm in charge, there'll be no more of that?* The dismissal in his voice evoked a rising belligerence from her; to prevent argument—

"I got Mummy a television set, a monster," she changed the subject with cowardly abruptness. "She was thrilled."

"Yes," was all he said, yet in the monosyllable did she hear a disparaging *Yes, I'd expect your mother's type to dote on the telly . . . ?*

She was silent a moment, then told herself resolutely,

29

Quit reading so much into every syllable of his. Good heavens, all he said was yes.

"Tired?" he murmured now. His eyes left his driving for another instant, to turn upon her a certain look that he did particularly well; it shed on her the fact of her own power of pleasing, of her effect on him, of his enjoyment—a sensual enjoyment—in being with her. As always this look, with its warming and melting flattery, dissipated the vague multitude of her apprehensions.

"No," she responded fervently and with gratitude. "I'm not the least bit tired." Abruptly she moved closer to him; he bent his head without turning it and rubbed his cheek against hers. The nuzzling caress held her in a moment of reassurance, not exactly happiness, but a prospect untroubled and pleasant and hopeful, even rather sweet.

They arrived at about five o'clock. From her first glance, as they drove between the two high gateposts topped by heraldic beasts weathered to anonymity, she did not doubt that she was in Elysium, but an Elysium she had never heard of. A gentle wind of road through green velvet, wide-spreading, brought them presently to a rambling survivor from another age, with a balustraded terrace all along it and a settled, placid, domestic look; at intervals its front was masked by heavy waterfalls of clematis in flower, only partly concealing a patchwork of styles of which the earliest was Jacobean and the latest Georgian. It was not a hotel but a superb old country house divided into suites, whose owners ran it more as a hobby than a profession. This did not prevent the charges from being astronomical, which made no difference to the clientele they sought to please; the people who knew of it kept their knowledge within a jealous, tightly closed circle, and indeed outsiders were not encouraged to come.

A very superior man-servant convoyed them and their luggage up a wide noble staircase with shallow treads. Their suite of two bedrooms (hers with dressing-room), two bathrooms, and small sitting-room were on the first floor. Auriol's room had a charming four-poster with hangings in sunny yellow silk; ancient flower tiles with their soft dim look surrounded a grate with a fire ready-laid but not lit, for the day was mild. Through every window were vistas of silent green, vast spaces that invited and released the spirit. When Ivor tapped lightly on her door she came out, and together they went down to a long panelled drawing-room and were met by all the ravishments of paper-thin bread-and-butter, home-made apricot jam and cakes of subtle invention; her husband disdained everything except two cups of tea, but Auriol demolished the lot, having had nothing since morning coffee. Two other couples were similarly engaged; they and Ivor had exchanged nods, but evidently—to her relief—there was to be no attempt at mingling. The owners of the place were not in evidence, and actually, during their stay, never appeared from first to last.

After tea they went out and walked leisurely arm-in-arm; Ivor knew the place well. Behind the house was an incredibly beautiful stable-block in perfect preservation enclosing a paved court and surmounted by a clock-tower. Some of it was converted to garages, but down along one whole side half-doors were open and horses' heads looked out, and in a distant paddock a rider and his mount went flying over a five-barred gate; saddle horses could always be had, Ivor explained, and rides could be quite extensive without the necessity for going outside the gates, since the domain comprised its own woods, meadows, farm, and a fair-sized ornamental water. As they wandered out of the stable-block the clock went six in a flat voice, an old, shaky, melancholy stroke. She halted a moment, trying to imagine the people who had moved to its bidding two hundred years ago, but perhaps then it had sounded more robust. It was like Ivor to have a place like this up his sleeve; if anything good were going—anything superlative, beautiful, sybaritic—he was sure to be on to it.

Then once more they separated; she had a rest and a long, luxurious, red-hot bath, and later on was regarding a girl in the full-length mirror with undeniable pleasure. It was a qualified pleasure with no triumph in it, no joy, no uplifted hard-beating heart for anticipation of a desired presence, of a being whose mere coming through a door could turn her dizzy . . . at once she beat off the hovering moth's wing of desolation, straightening herself with a sort of defiance. It was no good thinking of that, she was here in the present moment. And she was young and shapely with an unflawed throat, she was bathed and perfumed and strikingly attractive in a dashing dress of rather extreme style which suited her and which she carried off with an air; it was nice to think that an attractive man would take her in to dinner, and why had she thought *attractive man* and not *husband?* This time she was ready first, but somehow hesitated about tapping at his door. Instead she went down to wait for him, fresh and fragrant as a rose, her ankles and high-instepped feet graceful on the steps, her fingertips just touching the banister and making an exquisite line of arm against the old lustrous wood.

Dinner was in another panelled room where candlelight, so much more breathing than other light, made its faint pulsations on old honey-coloured oak. The tables were far apart; a butler in attendance was flanked by two smart maids; the food was as might be expected, very simple and so good it could not be better. The highlight was a bottle of Château Batailly, a claret dry yet soft as silk and with absolutely no lurking harshness to overtake the palate, a wine, of utter amiability and breeding. The first glass of this Ivor raised, waiting till she had done likewise; with eyes smiling at her, his mouth shaped a kiss. Her lips responded in the same fashion, and genuinely, in that moment, the seduction in her smile and glance was willing and unforced. Without that elation which seems to limn people in love with a sort of incandescence, she yet presented the picture of a pleased and happy woman.

Daylight was long in these months; they asked for coffee on the terrace, and a perfect little tray of silver and delicate china followed them outside. They sipped the delicious burning stuff during a long, wordless silence. Her eyes, wandering tranquilly over the hushed green vastness about them, presently returned to him. At his look, a curious full stop took her, a check to the spirit. His gaze was not on the felicities all around and about them, but indrawn; not actually frowning but very nearly, he seemed to contemplate some troubled horizon. Then, becoming aware of her eyes on him, his face cleared all at once and he smiled, reaching out his hand to her. The moment left her feeling unaccountably timid, as though she had seen something not intended for her eyes; still, the slight constraint dissolved away almost at once. They continued to sit side by side, occasionally touching hands; the silver coffee-pot before them changed from brilliant to luminous, reflecting a gentler and gentler day. From the wide peace about them rose an evening smell of grass; on the wall of the house the big blossoms of the flowering clematis lost their differences of colour, white and violet, and glimmered with an identical light like stars.

4

When she was in love with Giles, they had slept together only at the beginning. This had not happened at random, but for reasons. At about the second month of their affair, they knew that they would marry. It was then that Giles had asked her, "Do you want children?"

"I'm not very child-minded," she answered promptly, "but I want your children."

"I hoped you'd say that. All right." He was decisive. "From now on, we'll give bed a miss, if you agree. I'd rather we weren't rushed into marriage because you're pregnant, neither do I like the alternative. An abortion's no pleasure for either of us. Does it sound reasonable?"

"Much too reasonable." She glanced at him half-smiling but rueful, and he laughed aloud.

"Look at me like that and I'll beat you," he said. "If we fall by the wayside we fall, and take the consequences. But I must have more money when we marry, in case you've got to quit working. I've a rise coming any time now, the quarantine shouldn't last too long. We're going to be together all our lives," he bore on stoutly, against the smile that continued to flicker alluringly just beneath her lips. "I'm only trying to look ahead a little. Quit making fun of me, you trollop," he commanded. "Help me."

They had fallen by the wayside, naturally, but not

often. "A creditable score," Giles had bragged, justifiably complacent. For that was the crux of the whole situation—the degree, the mere degree of their attraction for each other; the ruthless magnetism that merged and drowned their identities one in the other; the spell that purged them of their minds and gave them the boundless liberty of each other's bodies. And this mindlessness, the companion of rape which is its horror, when companioned by love is the great purifier. *Oh lust, Oh innocent thing*, often she remembered the words of an American poet; and it was innocent, that intent of love which is fusion, by what means achieved the lovers themselves hardly knew, and in which indecency or license are aggregates of sound without meaning. And this joint entrance into another world, where the body and mind are stripped of their everyday law and governance, was like being flung into the very heart of an unknown voltage, with something of the same helplessness and terror. And assuredly she and Giles deserved full marks for winning, most of the time, against such an adversary . . .

The memory of that urgency between herself and Giles spurred her to a realization: the absence of any comparable urgency between herself and Ivor, during the months of their acquaintance. It came as a shock; she had not imagined in herself such a depth of stupidity that it should catch up with her, fully, only on her wedding-night. Between her new husband and herself there had been an affability, a constantly caressing manner that had seemed—now she thought of it—to take the place of contact. Ivor caressed her not with his hands, but with his acquiescences, his smile, the inflections of his voice. Almost, they seemed to avoid touching each other . . . ? No, surely not; they were simply undemonstrative. But she had been very demonstrative, with Giles; even while he was driving her hand would lie on the seat so that the back of it brushed his thigh; constantly, if only through the contact of fingertips, they would reaffirm the imperiousness of the bond between them. And supposing it were for Giles that she undressed now, in this mirrored room, seeing the festive dress and delicate lace underthings slip off to reveal her body, pliant and shapely and with that luminousness which is the distant light of the buried scarlet stream, its brilliance screened by flesh into living cream and rose. Suppose it were for Giles that she would presently enter, with her offering of youth, beauty, and seduction, the lovely room that held the hush and repose and the wide bed . . .

Angrily, she pushed the thought away with both hands. She must stop making these deathly comparisons at every step; it was cruel to Ivor, grossly unfair and unjust, to say nothing of how crippling to her own state of mind and intention. Yet only now the knowledge impaled her—that what was over, was not over; that the scar took its own time about fading out, and was no more to be argued away than a scar on the body. At this new and unwelcome access of knowledge, she stared with consternation and misgiving.

A single small shaded lamp hardly illumined, but gently stroked, a visibility upon the darkness. From the bed she saw him, by this barely achieved light, come softly into the room. He approached the wide bed and leaned across the space that would hold him, putting his hand on her arm and whispering, "Auriol." She put up a hand and brushed it across his lips and cheek; he smiled faintly and straightened. She closed her eyes, in the next few moments hearing the faint susurration as he took off his dressing-gown and slippers, and was suddenly glad that she herself wore a delicate film of pleated silk; it would somehow have been a gaucherie, instinct told her, to have lain there naked against his coming. Now with eyes still closed she felt the bed taking his weight, and he came near to her, turning on his side and putting one arm under her head and the other around her waist. Responsively she turned toward him, and since one arm was pinioned against his chest she could clasp him only with the other. Then a breathing-space intervened, a long pause. After her long chill solitude it was by no means unpleasant to lie there, her whole length lightly held against a warm body with its faint fragrance of meticulous grooming, to feel the contrast between his male hard-muscled texture in its envelope of thin silk pajamas. A moment of content and reassurance enveloped her; he was very nice, if somewhat finicky and of unpredictable humour, but it was up to her to thread a negotiable path among his various quirks of mood and keep to it, to make their joint lives a success. If he would be affectionate she was more than ready to respond, if he would be passionate she was ready to be acquiescent, and smiling again, lulled, she tightened her arm around him and felt a pressure of his own arms, responsive but fleeting.

Another lapse of time intervened, another pause, before she awoke to a faint feeling of a crisis; a first crisis. This long, unemphatic embrace had outlived significance and validity, and had arrived at the point where it must merge into the next gesture. Only what? the essential pulse of love-making was a crescendo—perhaps delicate, perhaps gross, but at all events a crescendo. Instinctively apprehensive of let-down at this stage, she opened her eyes and glanced at him quickly, even furtively. He lay as if asleep, the faint smile still on his face, except that she felt uneasily it had passed from faint to enigmatic. Momentarily at a loss, she now realized that this next step must be of her providing. She flicked him with another uncertain, measuring glance; then gently, almost timidly, started to undo his pajama jacket. As the first couple of buttons laid bare the hollow of his throat she put her lips to it, burrowing in with imperious little thrusts, like a grazing kid.

"Yes," he murmured, "yes, yes," and when he began to stroke her she whispered, "Ivor, dear Ivor, dear dear Ivor," and put her free arm around his neck. They began to kiss, after the fashion in which he always kissed her, a sort of nibbling or nuzzling that brushed the outer boundaries of desire and then somehow (or as far as she was concerned) fell short, and always in the same way: first she found it titillating, then faintly unpleasant, and finally she experienced a desire to pull away brusquely with a cheated, exhausted feeling. Yet to pull away now, of all times, was as out of the question as brusqueness, and in the same moment she realized that this passage of kissing, like the other, was running out to its end in a dying fall instead of lifting and carrying them to the next plane. Forcibly, as though insisting on her goodwill in all this, she freed her imprisoned left arm, took his hand and carried it to her breast. He gave a caressing murmur of acquiescence, and with both her hands, one on either side of his waist, she began to trace with a silken touch the upward curve of his body, and felt him nestle more closely against her. A thankfulness pervaded her, and simultaneously a reminder: that she had no knowledge whatever of his sexual . . . pace, would one call it? gait, tempo . . . ? That there must be infinite differences in men she accepted readily, except that her own experience—to negligible affairs without intimacy, then Giles—had not equipped her with that comprehensive a bird's-eye view. But a man naturally reticent, perhaps a trifle over-refined, would hardly make love like a ditch-digger. Ivor was very graceful for a man, with a feline unhurriedness of movement; perhaps after all it was natural to him, this mannered, deliberate prolongation? . . . In the same instant she felt, unmistakably, the small ground-swell of emotion slipping away, and realized with something like panic that this achieved point of momentum was crucial, that at all costs she must not let it fall back. Yet since he lay there passive as a sultana, it was all in her hands; from step to step, palpably, the initiative was up to her, and a dawning sense of burden was joined by something sharper— exasperation. And now, what next? Get down to it, obviously. The bare-fisted phrase started a desolate, irresistible amusement deep within her, in the same moment that her mind fingered the tied silk drawstring around his waist as the next point of approach. But her hand, almost before it started moving toward him, stopped. She was timid, constrained; to tell the truth, she dared not venture on such a liberty without either an unmistakable invitation or a prelude of much more fervor than they had been able to generate. And if it were ridiculous, still that was the effect he had on her.

He was saying something; it was startling, almost, he had been so inanimate. She had missed it through unreadiness, for the words were perfectly indistinguishable. Bending, she brought her head against his, and with her lips touching the lobe of his ear she breathed, "What? What did you say?"

The murmuring came from him again, and now she was close enough to tell, almost certainly, that it was not language. It was sound, inarticulate sound, yet unmistakably conveying not only a desire of some sort but an actual command, imperious. At a loss, feeling that she should be able to interpret it but perfectly unable to do so, she pressed her head even closer against him, straining with every nerve to catch any syllable, anything to give her a clue. Between herself and Giles had been plenty of this sort of communication of love uttered but never spoken, sounds on the verge of words but never needing to condense into words, and their every faintest signal from one to the other was a flare in the dark, a signal rocket of white fire to the most hidden wish. And the contrast between that lightning telepathy and this halting labour, every step of it crippled by constraint and calculation, overwhelmed her with sudden disgust and anger—but disgust mostly for herself, anger at her ineptness and failure of interpretation. In the same moment she realized for how much time this clumsy groping had been going on, how long and exhaustingly it had spun itself out and how fatally it was draining her of physical and nervous strength. And of courage . . .

His lips were still moving, more and more soundlessly; with a final effort she supplicated in a whisper, "Tell me, tell me." But again he lay passive, only now he held her with a perceptible relaxing of his arms. At the same time his expression changed, the faint smile unaltered, but transformed—by that fluid magic of feature requiring no movement whatever—from complaisant to sardonic. This again passed in a flash to inscrutable, or was it merely the reflection of her own anxiety? An access of alarm overtook her, a frightened conviction that matters must not rest here, that somehow she must spur the laggard moment to some next point, and with a movement too sharp and nervous she touched the tied silk cord, again hesitated, then compromised by moving her hand downward from his waist over the silk, in a gently stroking movement. At once and unmistakably he responded with a negative headshake; her head had been lying on his chest, but she raised it in time to see the flicker of a frown appear between his brows and vanish. She gaped, impaled on separate thorns of embarrassment, awkwardness, and incomprehension while her hand, not arrested soon enough, moved by reflex in the same caress. Again and at once he shook his head, this time strongly, in the same moment taking her hand and decisively imprisoning it under his arm, while he forced her head to the pillow again and into the hollow of his neck and shoulder.

Pinioned in this repose, half by force and half by fatigue, she lay for a long few moments in a suspension, motionless and blank. What had just happened she could not have said, what performance had been expected of her she had no idea. By all means then, she was clumsy, inept, a bungler. The cold-blooded substitution of skill for love was beyond her; her training was bad, it had been in love but not in skill. If she felt anything in that moment beside bafflement, it was . . . injury, that was it; she felt injured that her tacit complaisance and acquiescence had not been enough. And if not enough, still she had offered what she could and could offer no more at the moment . . .

"Tired?" he murmured, just above her ear, and an

unqualified *Yes* almost got away from her. By good fortune she was able to catch it in time and substitute, deprecatingly, "A little."

He was silent long enough to make her look at him questioningly, from her niche in his shoulder having to cast her eyes upward—just in time to meet his own eyes which had opened full for a moment then closed at once, after darting at her a single glance. So unmistakable and unqualified was the mockery in this glance that it startled her into a new speechlessness; lying against him, she had the sensation of having to catch her breath from shock. But again he was murmuring, "Go to sleep." His arm held her closer and she felt this pressure as more peremptory than affectionate. "Hush, hush," his voice went on like a spell, more tenuous than a whisper, "hush, go to sleep," and she closed her eyes obediently and lay rigid, a thousand miles from sleep. Uneasiness enclosed her like a cobweb, each filament as sharp and binding as wire. *Animals are cleaner,* she thought suddenly. *One thing's to be done and it's done and over with, none of these elaborate preambles and horrible unspoken reservations, the thousand things that can't be said . . .*

A balm, unexpected, fell upon her unrest and resentment; Ivor's lips brushed across her forehead. His mouth felt smooth and cool, quite untouched by the heat of a kiss. *Chaste,* sneered something within her, deep down. *We're a fine pair.* Yet all the same there spread through her not only the extreme of relief, but a boundless gratitude. Without words he had signalled that they were friends, that he did not hold the failure against her. The reassurance, of course, had been light and fleeting. Perfunctory? maybe. She would not bargain with the quality of the caress; she had to take comfort where she found it. And she took it eagerly, grasping it, the tension going out of her a little and then with a rush, completely. With thankfulness she gave herself up to languor, delicious, nestling to him with a long sigh and letting her arm drop across his waist, a gesture he did not reject. Heavenly to give over for a while all that effort and constraint, delicious to lie there, a blank, conscious of nothing but the pleasure of warmth and closeness. Understanding her husband as incompletely as she did, it could hardly occur to her the mere degree of her relaxation against him told him all he needed to know; that of her thankful abandonment to passivity, not one nuance had escaped him—to be stored up in the recesses of his temperament and to emerge in its own good time as something transformed beyond recognition. Those had been the days of her innocence, her complete innocence of Ivor Hailes's secret geography. Innocent, she went to sleep in the curve of his arm, her face against his neck and shoulder. Above her sleeping face lay motionless, likewise, his own mask of sleep; comely, enigmatic, with something brushed across his lips that might—or might not be—the faintest smile.

At a period of time later, she had been roused by some indefinable cause. By no means thoroughly awake, she realized what it was: Ivor freeing himself, very gently and cautiously, from their sleeping involvement. At once, with that strange play of instinct that remains constant, even in moments submerged or half-submerged, she knew that he wanted her to remain asleep and that he was taking extraordinary pains to that end, holding down the edge of the mattress against its rebound, as he slid off the bed. Then there was a silence, unbroken by any sound of departing footsteps. She felt that he stood watching her, and now she deliberately simulated the calm and imperceptible breathing of sleep; after a few moments she heard him go. The moment of duplicity stroked her briefly with unease, as if she had performed some contemptible deceit. Against this vague guilt, as antidote, she lay thinking that when he returned she would pretend to wake suddenly. She would turn toward him, throw her arms about him, see if the warmth of this greeting might not kindle something between them to efface the chill of the other failure. Trying to enact in advance her exact degree of fervour and what words she would use, presently she drifted again into the cumulus cloud of sleep, with its piled wool of comfort and forgetfulness.

The next time she woke it was with a start, for no reason apparent to her. The room was barely visible in this predawn light, like a reflection in dark water; her eyes roamed it muzzily, then with more focus. She was alone. A good deal of time must have passed since Ivor had gone, some hours in fact; he had not merely left the room for a few moments, as she had supposed. Pushed by an anxiety sudden but formless she slipped out of bed, went to the door. He had closed it behind him, though so softly she had heard nothing. Passing barefoot over the carpeted square hallway of the suite she reached his door, then stopped dead. To knock at this hour and under these circumstances was peculiar, if not ludicrous, and she had the right to walk in if she chose, yet to exercise this right was somehow doubtful.

In compromise, and hardly aware, she took the doorknob in a tight hold lest it should rattle. It was firm and moved like velvet, in this house doorknobs did not rattle, but she had had to be sure. Then—all at once—she realized something; she had expected to find the door locked. Hard upon this misgiving she saw it moving soundlessly past the jamb, so it was not locked. With utmost stealth she widened the crack and, rather short of breath, peered in. He was in the wide bed, another four-poster, his back turned to her, his dark head half out of sight in the pillow; the slow calm respiration of sleep became evident to her as she stood there, yet she herself had counterfeited the same effect not long ago. Was he really asleep? or pretending to be, . . . all the time aware of her?

After a long moment she closed the door again with painfullest care, soundlessly padding back to bed. The incident had knocked her into full wakefulness, and lying wide-eyed in the half dark she gave herself over to thought on the situation. She had married a man who was undemonstrative, apparently; a man slow to respond to the persuasion of commonplace endearments. It was an odd picture, his leaving her alone like that; not for a short while, but for the night. And this abandonment had in it an atmosphere so special that she found herself searching for the precise word to describe it, as if this preciseness might explain everything with final clarity. Was it rejection? no. Disappointment? no. Was it resentment, pique, anger? no . . . the right word suddenly came to her, at once anticlimactic yet crushing: discard. He had walked away from her as from a discarded newspaper, once and for all of no further use. Then her common sense rose to dispute the simile. He might be annoyed at the episode, but why blame her? She had been willing, unmistakably willing; on this point her conscience and self-approbation were clear and aggressive. If anyone were to blame, it was not she . . . then decisively she abandoned this line of thought for practical reassurance. This same thing happened to many married people, without affecting their lives afterward. She was disturbing herself needlessly over some impasse of this particular temperament, a temperament (as it happened) more unknown to her than she had imagined. Well, she would learn to know it. If its springs were deeply hidden she would explore gently, cautiously, till she found them. This abortive wedding-night was not the end of everything, next time she would think of something . . .

Reassurance, confirmed, fell over her like an extra blanket on a chill night. She was sleepy again; it felt good, to be sleepy. She yawned; it was delicious to yawn, and presently she would be hungry, and it was wonderful to be hungry. The mere mechanical life of the healthy body was bliss in itself, to be taken with no small gratitude. Half-smiling with restored confidence, a new possibility overtook her, of a support and confidence even more lulling. It might be that she had married a clever, amusing, agreeable companion who was sexually undemanding. The thought was so wonderful that she rushed to welcome it. But along with this con-currence she refused—with a strange cowardice—to let the inevitable corollary take shape, even in her mind: that if she were right in this estimate of Ivor, she could be married to him without being unfaithful to Giles.

5

"Were you angry with me last night?"

"Angry with you? why would I be angry with you?"

"Well, I mean—did I do anything? I mean, anything to—to offend you, anything wrong?"

"My dear child! what an idea."

"Well, but I mean"—held at arm's length, she persisted more and more awkwardly—"your leaving me. I mean, alone like that—"

"My sweet, what of it? my deplorable bachelor habits." His dark lazy glance rallied her indulgently. "I can't rest properly two in a bed, even when you're the other. If I'm to sleep, I must be alone."

"But I mean"—still, and clumsily, she strove against the enigma—"I must have done something wrong that you'd leave me like that, and I'd so much rather you'd tell me straight out what it was than circle around it—"

"I'm circling around nothing, and there's nothing to tell you. It was two or three in the morning and I thought we'd better sleep, both of us." The very faint impatience in his tone subsided to a negligence. "Fancy your making a thing of it."

"Sorry if I seem to make a thing of it," she answered coldly, but her mind was not working at all; it was urgent that something further be said, but he had deprived her of the ability to think.

"Well, perhaps not a thing. An atmosphere." He smiled. "Lord, how I hate atmospheres. And how did you, in fact"—he was polite, solicitous—"sleep?"

"Very well, thanks." By some sleight-of-hand she could not follow he had compelled her to this flaccid house-party exchange. "And you?"

"Oh! splendidly, thanks. Total oblivion the moment my head touched the pillow." The smile he gave her was now touched (she was sure of it) with mockery. "And what would you like to do this morning, my love? anything special?"

That exchange on the terrace, all morning sun, country airs, and waterfalls of clematis, was her first taste of his gift—not only for holding her at bay, but of reducing her to ineptitude, even to a sort of loutishness, yet she had never considered herself inept or a lout. This consideration, which would in time become important, was at the moment unimportant. Just now it was he who overwhelmed her, he and his manner that asserted everything between them was as it should be, and dared her to say the opposite. Confronted by this falseness she was too overcome with bewilderment, just then, to feel it as monstrous. And in this rented room where she now sat, amid the rubbed-out mean furniture used by a succession of transients, she still flinched from other memories, countless, of his ability to mock her, to slide away from her every attempt to come to grips with fact, and to reduce her to that floundering gaucherie so completely fatal to thought and articulateness, and still more fatal to their situation—she felt clamorously—than actual dissension. In any passage of words between them, she was lost in advance. It had taken her a long time to accept this, and likewise accept that having right and logic on her side did her no good at all. For his agility of word and thought (unclean, she came to regard it in time) she was no match; at will he could make her look all kinds of a fool. Her remembrance of these encounters was somehow more searing than her remembrance of bodies encountering, bodies seldom naked

47

(he was oddly reserved about nakedness, though in her arms she could feel him strong and well shaped and though slight, elegantly slight), during which her education continued, progressively more humiliating and dismaying. She was to learn his enigmatic veerings of mood, his capriciousness, his exactions that he would not make plain; she came to the fullest understanding that the mockery which could disintegrate her on a terrace or in a room lost nothing of its deadliness by being transferred to bed. The climax of all this—the impaling spike—was the single time, very recent, that he had whispered to her, "Don't let me fail!" Before that fierce appeal she perceived, for once and all, her bankruptcy. She had in her nothing with which to respond, not even a simulated fervour; she had spent herself during a series of defeating nights, and recognized at last exactly what she was: a woman of normal emotion, up against something she could not handle. Misery takes strange forms, and at the most sunken pitch of hers it was an evocation from *L'Après-Midi* that swam and trembled fitfully in her exhausted mind, the thing dimly seen moving in the dim forest tangle, the faun cruel and graceful, not human. Or not quite human, or at least not recognizably human . . .

All this intricate prelude was the threshold to a single, stark fact: that in eight months of marriage she had not once gone to bed successfully with her husband.

"Oh! the plane was indescribable, marvelous, stupendous. Flying's a commonplace? Not to me, and never will be, never, never. My God, to walk to that thing the size of a row of houses, and know it's going to get five miles up in the air! And over Gander the clouds, oh my God, black and in savage shapes like axe-blades and prows of Viking ships, and along their edges pour the Northern Lights! And oh Christ, flying back to England and the sunrise, and the whole firmament divided exactly in half by day and night! Behind you darkness and

48

stars, and ahead of you the dawn, oh God, even I could worship!"

Having blown off her incongruous top layer of poetry like the froth off beer, Maggie descended to more natural levels.

"And the plane full of rancid silly voices, all of them nattering and not one with glance to spare for the miracles going on outside, oh God! And what happened to Sid Gross's show while I was away?" Maggie's swooping digressions were an old story to Auriol. "Don't tell me, I read all about it in dear old New York." She grinned wolfishly. "I knew that little bitch wouldn't hold up, no real quality, no core, no guts, and it's cost Sid a pretty packet to find it out. She fooled everybody," Maggie summed up complacently. "Everybody but me,

"A human divining-rod," said Ivor dulcetly, and at once Auriol was nervous; dulcetness, with him, never boded any good. "How awe-inspiring."

"Well, it comes useful in my trade," Maggie said unabashed. "A producer sends to you for a type you mustn't be pat, yet all the same you must hit the nail on the head."

"As a hitter of nails, I can believe in you," Ivor acclaimed. "Implicitly, Miss Bolter."

"Miss Bolter!" Maggie turned a smile, not altogether easy, on Auriol. "Did you ever, Roly? how long is it since anyone's called me that? Maggie," she exhorted, turning to Ivor. "Join the mob-scene and call me Maggie."

"But if I happen not to care for mob-scenes? No, I decline to sully my lips with Maggie. Come, you must have a proper label, you weren't *christened* Maggie, were you? And not Margaret either, something tells me," he pursued suavely, against her silence. "Tell us the worst."

"Well"—Maggie's assumption of entering robustly into the jest was a bit hollow—"as a matter of fact . . . Maybelle."

"With two *ll*'s?" Ivor nodded sapiently. "I knew it. Well, you were in a cleft stick, weren't you? between Maybelle and Mabe." His grimace was faint but eloquent. "By comparison even Maggie was preferable, wasn't it? I do see your position."

"I don't blame you for hating Maggie," said Maggie, with good-fellowship slightly forced. "I hate it myself."

"I hate all nicknames," said Ivor. His articulation was over-clear, another danger signal Auriol recognized by now. "Most of them are either offensive or silly. Names have a life of their own, did it ever strike you? Take Dorothy, for instance—an acceptable name, beautiful even. But if the woman's silly or trivial or otherwise insignificant, inevitably she'll become Dot. Dot Osborne! Dot Sayers! can you imagine? No, no." He shuddered theatrically. "There's destiny in names, too much destiny for comfort. Now, take women with a certain rough-hewn type of name, they're almost bound to be 'earty. It's their fate, they can't escape, Women with names like Mame. Or . . . "

"Or Maggie?" the name's proprietor injected, into his delicate pause.

More delicately still, Ivor murmured, "If you say so."

"I said it for you," Maggie challenged. The signals of warfare were kindling in her eyes and voice and on her cheekbones, yet at once she had hold of herself. Auriol, looking on in a humiliation that lamed her power to interpose, knew that this self-control was for her sake. "I heard it, no fear."

"Oh, but you're very sensitive," Ivor's tone drowsed. "To American voices, for example. Of course," he observed, even more dreamily, "we never know our own voices—we've no idea, usually, how we sound. By the way, Auriol once told me that you did the casting for *One Sardine, Nearly New?*"

"I—" Maggie, thrown off by the digression, visibly lost her grip on the new elements of resentment she was gathering. "Yes, actually, I did."

"A triumph," Ivor assured her. "A triumph of obviousness. Hit the nail on the head by all means, but don't necessarily bludgeon it. Or don't you agree?"

"I do," said Maggie collectedly. "I do agree." Visibly, to Auriol's sight and understanding, she had put away anger and the impulse to strike back, and now wore an uncharacteristic look of dignity and composure. A creditable performance for a woman essentially aggressive and quick-tempered, and whether she could have faced up to him effectually did not make it any the less admirable. What an effort it must have cost her, to swallow his baiting and repeated small insults in which the wit might not be devastating, but the intention was. And again Auriol knew why Maggie did it; it was all for her, to spare her.

"I'd better pop along," Maggie was saying, and Ivor's murmur of, "Oh Maybelle, must you?" had the accent of the tormentor balked of his prey. Also, by some legerdemain of nuance, he made the two *ll*'s in the name audible.

"I'm sorry," Auriol blurted at the door. "I'm so, so—"

"It's all right," Maggie soothed her. "It's all right."

"No, no," Auriol besought. Her throat felt sore; tears were not actually in her eyes, but anything would put them there. Unbearable to see loud-mouthed effervescent Maggie snubbed and cancelled; to see her rattled and unsure of herself, all her ebullience quenched. "Don't mind though, *please* don't mind—"

"I don't," said Maggie. "I don't mind."

"I—I—I—" Auriol struggled on.

"Hush then," said Maggie. "Roly love, don't give it a thought. It's nothing."

It was only much later that the expression in Maggie's eyes struck Auriol as less eloquent of hurt for Maggie than of compassion for Auriol. At the moment she was only aware of her heartbreak for the pathos of Maggie's not daring, while saying good-bye in Ivor's presence, to address her as Roly.

Silent, she re-entered the drawing-room. Ivor sat in a pleasurable raptness, like a canary-gorged cat. After a couple of moments her failure to speak must surely be noticeable, yet when he uttered—in his own good time —it was without the least hint of constraint.

"Curious people you do collect, my sweet, as I've said before," he observed. "It's kind of you, but unlimited kindness isn't practicable."

"I'm doing Maggie no kindness by knowing her, I assure you," she retorted a little too loudly. "If anything, it's the other way around."

"Come, come, my love."

"She's a marvelous woman." Instantly she wished she had not said *marvelous*; as a disemboweller of superlatives, Ivor was unequalled. "Her way of talking, it's an absolute disguise, it's a—a contradiction of what she really is. I know her," she asseverated, with a horrid knowledge that the more she insisted, the weaker she sounded. "I've known her twelve years, and you don't know her in the least. And I wish it hadn't been like this, that's all." Again her desire to cry was a treachery that must be fought. "I wish things hadn't happened like this."

"Happened?" His calm eyes turned more fully upon her, opening wider in question. "Did anything happen? when?"

Staggered, she could only goggle at him. It was this power of his that undid her, as it had from her first perception of it; his power to foment a detestable and perilous atmosphere and then, wide-eyed and ingenuous, disclaim its very existence. Under this disavowal her grasp on the situation disappeared, together with all her faculties of thought and speech; she was too busy scrabbling for a handhold on the plunging slides of his duplicity. But in those early days she had refused to give up, and that was her defeat; she argued and fought on fiercely, losing ground all the time and being reduced, finally, to impotent stammering. Certainly before long she learned not to give him the chance to laugh at her, but this had been one of the occasions when she would not strike her flag.

"It's the first time she's been here," she persisted. Maggie's departure from her home was vivid before her eyes; at any moment her voice and mouth must take the shape of a sob. "The very first time, and you couldn't even—"

"These idiotic distinctions," he cut her off waspishly. "The first or the fiftieth time, what's that to do with it? Or"—he added, with new and weighted significance—"or with what she is? As flagrant a type as I've ever seen."

"She—she's not. She—"

"Who could miss it? Don't, I beg you," he adjured, "be that innocent. Or that obtuse, if you like."

Her first silence, defeated, was succeeded by a silence quite different. She was rallying, gathering her scattered forces about her.

"She may be what you're hinting," she began doggedly. "In her private life, she may be. All I can tell you is, that so far as I'm concerned—I mean, her behaviour to me—there's never been a trace of it. And I've been alone with her at her country cottage—"

"Madness," he ejaculated under his breath. "Sheer madness."

"—also with other people," she bore on stubbornly, "and there was *nothing* that pointed that way, nothing at all. And if it exists"—she shrugged—"it's certainly no affair of mine."

"Disclaim it if you like," he invited. "You can't disclaim the impression she makes—the general effect. To tell you the truth"—he made the infinitesimal pause that usually preceded one of his body-blows—"I wondered at your associating with her. I found it perfectly extraordinary, not to say reckless. If I hadn't been out with you a few times before that, it might have put me right off. Didn't you ever realize you might be tarred with the same brush? didn't it ever occur to you?"

Transfixed for a moment, she found she had to stop and think.

"I've forgotten long ago what—what she looks like," she groped, finally. "I only know you don't give up that sort of friend, if you've got one. So what you just said" —her voice stiffened—"no, it didn't occur to me."

"Didn't occur! and it doesn't occur to you now?"

"No," she flung at him hardily. "And what's more I don't believe there's a word of truth in your insinuations, not one."

"No?" he smiled. "Tell that to most people, and see if they'd agree with you."

"Most people," she mocked. He seldom gave her such an opening, and she leaped at it. "Since when do you go by the opinions of 'most people'? You amaze me." Her gibing tone was unwise, no one knew it better than she, but she was apt to lean too hard on these rare opportunities. "Despising everyone as you do—you astonish me, really. 'Most people.' Hah!"

His face tightened ominously; her ascendancy, however fleeting, was the one thing he could not endure at all. The geniality overspread him, equally ominous, and she knew he had found means of reprisal.

"At the best," he said smoothly, "the woman's a costermonger, a buttonless Pearly Queen." This was so harmless compared to her anticipation that she started to draw breath, then saw that the finishing stroke was yet to be delivered. "In any case," he pursued, "I've never understood this business of people being shaken because one doesn't yearn over their friends. *I was so sure you'd like so and so, and you don't.* Idiotic. Everyone can't like everyone else, can they?" He paused, his look of geniality deepening; she understood that whatever came next, was the poison. "For example, your mamma doesn't like me, yet do I complain?"

A fatigue, total, descended on her like blackout. Neither could she undertake to debate with him the precise shadings—the positives or negatives—of her mother's regard for himself. The gauntlet he had thrown down was mere derision, an underlining of his supreme indifference to his mother-in-law's sentiments, whether of affection or otherwise. Mrs. Chapman was not more given to unstitched talk about trifles than most women of her age, but how Ivor must assess her, Mrs. Chapman's daughter could easily imagine.

"We'll wash it off—having Mummy to dinner tomorrow night," she blurted foolishly. "We'd better cancel it."

"Cancel it? but what for?" His eyebrows were innocent and hurt. "When I'm looking forward to it so much? My sweet, by no means."

What he meant (of course) was that Mrs. Chapman was such poor game for his shafts that his wife need not be uneasy about his behaviour tomorrow evening.

Mrs. Chapman's daughter understood that too.

6

Affairs moved into their final and shattering phase some weeks later. They had separate rooms, but at the moment were in bed together. Such occasions, not frequent but by no means non-existent, were never of her seeking; with shrinking nerves and body painfully tensed she would listen to his approach, and the sound of his slippered feet made her think of a padding animal in the dark. Then it would begin again, the sterile advances forever arriving nowhere, forever falling short of the goal. Moreover, these encounters of the night had now taken on a different character. When Ivor was in bed with her she felt him, obscurely, an enemy. He had become rough, erratic, capricious, and she knew that this was calculated and deliberate; often he hurt her, and at her cry never failed with the silkiest apology, yet his face in the dim lamplight had a satyr's amusement, wicked; almost she expected to see the faun's ears prick up at either side of his head. In a certain special way, he was inflicting retaliation upon her. With each of his entrances into her bed he was giving her a new chance in the certain and malicious knowledge of her failure, and at the end of their exhausting futile commerce he would punish her with these spiteful hurts, his manner suggesting that he could do worse if he had a mind to; it was exactly like being with an animal whose playfulness, too easily, crosses the hairline into viciousness. While vividly aware of this, she cultivated a deliberate obliviousness. She was not beaten yet; to confess herself beaten was the final epitaph on their marriage, and stubbornly she rejected it. One day she would find something to unlock the maddening enigmatic door and save the two of them, she would think of *something*. Except that, at this point, she was still obtuse about realizing one thing: that virtuosity in the act of love was not a conscious thing to be attained at will or even recollected at will, having been struck off in the white heat of the moment, fresh and perfect and unique, mostly as irrecoverable as those ancient porcelains of which no modern potter can tell how they were done—something that remains a secret of the furnace.

This particular time had been at the end of one of their desolating rendezvous. After them she always felt stale and pawed and would like to plunge quickly into a bath, but dared not; it would be too pointed. Accordingly they were still lying awake side by side with eyes wide open, yet not looking at each other. It was then that he spoke; no question, but a statement.

"You were engaged to be married, before we met."

"Yes," she said at once. Hesitation she would not traffic in, for to hesitate would be to repudiate Giles. Within her, all the same, arose a silent clamour of fear, a sense of new and unpredictable danger.

"How many times?"

"Just the one."

"Yes, that's—"

He checked himself at once, but she heard the unspoken, *Yes that's what I've heard,* and understood that he had been finding out about her—from the gossip area, of course, made up of what individuals she could only guess . . .

"Why?" he was continuing. "You were nearly twenty-eight when we married. Why only one engagement?"

She was silent a moment, then said lamely, "I expect it just happened so."

"Oh no," he countered, with ominous affability. "You're much too desirable to've got to the late twenties without attracting a lot of men. Why haven't you a string of scalps to your credit, instead of one lone engagement? And why?"—he made one of his feline pounces—"why did you frown, just then? because"—he answered his own question—"you don't like me to talk about the sacred betrothal."

She was still silent, not only from resentment, but from a still worse cowardice; she felt that her chances of saying something wrong—irremediably wrong—were infinite, and literally she dared not speak, to invite God knew what alienation.

"Tell me." His voice achieved paradox; it had turned coaxing, but remained mocking. "Tell me why you were only engaged the one time."

"Oh Lord," she struck out, wanting to break from the impasse on any terms. "I expect because—because I wasn't in love before, not really in love."

"But this time"—he paused infinitesimally—"you were."

"Yes."

"You were in love."

"Yes."

"His name was Giles something, I've forgotten."

"Kelvin," she said after a moment.

"Yes," he murmured. In his tone was a satisfaction, as though he had extorted some damaging admission. A long moment elapsed, of inscrutable character, during which her eyes closed and her mind suspended itself for a moment. Sheathed in the precarious safeguard of this blankness, she felt only one thing: dread of what was coming next. The next thing, as a matter of fact, was his freeing himself from the covers and rising. The movement, much more abrupt than usual with him, made her open her eyes. He was standing just beside the bed, looking down on her. Upon his face, before he left, was

58

the faintest cryptic something that suggested to her not good night, but a final leave-taking.

Yet, next night he came to her room again. A sequence of two nights running was in any case unusual, and also they had dined with friends (his friends) and come in late, and his mood throughout the evening had been dark and rather preoccupied; his hosts had asked him if he were tired, and he admitted to being very tired. It seemed likewise that she was tired enough not to have heard him approach; when the door opened, she had not meant to turn her head so sharply toward it and stare at him wide-eyed, but the movement had been surprised out of her. At once she was struck by a difference in his manner. The air of sombre fatigue was gone, and replaced by—of all things—a glistening good-fellowship. And in this highly varnished camaraderie was much mockery, such burlesque of amiability, that it turned her literally cold. Her first confused thought—that she must be ready—was shouldered by the next question: ready for what? Mistrustful, motionless, yet trying to assume an ordinary amiable look, she watched him as he took off his dressing-gown and slippers (he always appeared before her correctly clad), moved the blankets, and disposed his elegant and well-made length beside her.

She smiled at him, pretending to be drowsy, and he smiled at her. A long pause ensued, during which he made not the least attempt to touch her. Merely at a loss for any other expedient she closed her eyes, her profile toward him, then actually drowsed a little, was drifting off . . . she woke all at once, for no reason; no touch or word of his had roused her. Turning her head, she met his eyes full. He was no nearer than at first, lying on his side and regarding her in a manner peculiarly wide-awake. Again he smiled, with that improbable amiability, and said, "Are you sleepy?" in a slumbrous, lulling voice unpleasantly a variance with his intensely awake look, and which she knew to be another indication ominous of its kind; by now she had mastered quite a gamut of these danger signals.

"Oh no," she disclaimed. Wariness clogged her, the fear of putting a foot wrong. "Not really. I thought," she ventured, "that *you* were tired."

"You'd rather I went?" he asked quickly, and more quickly—too quickly—she protested, "No, no." (That habit of his, that clapping of an interpretation on her words, from whose entrapment she must disengage herself strand by strand, a fly struggling from a web . . .) "You—it's just that you said you were tired, earlier on," she continued haltingly. "You told Stephen so."

"I'm always tired when I'm bored," he returned. "What yapping, my God, what talk."

"They're your friends," she pointed out, with a degree of satisfaction.

"Business, my angel," he pointed out in his turn, "forces one to herd with uncongenial growths. But you, so far as I know, are under no such compulsion." His tone, of dulcet implication, raised up between them the image of Maggie as a witness to her bad taste. While she was registering this—

"Tell me about Giles," he said without preamble. The turn of subject was so unforeseen that her mouth hung open for an instant before she snapped it shut.

"See here," she began with a sort of violence, and stopped. That her anger should evoke his had been her immediate apprehension, but nothing of the sort happened; he merely lay looking at her with that unimpaired amiability as he returned, "See what?—Do go on," he besought, as she lay silent. "Tell me what it is I'm to see. I await revelation." As he spoke she had abandoned her resistance, obeying some urge of expediency, and now lay waiting in a tight submission for what might come.

"Was he tall?" the inquisition resumed, as if nothing had broken it.

"Medium tall."

"Strongly built?"

"Yes, very."

"Masculine?"

"Yes."

"Able? potent? virile?"

The silence that followed was more dangerous than any answer, freighted as it was with her unspoken retort, *If you'd been capable of finding out, you'd know how long it's been since I've touched a man.* He heard it too, if not word for word then the gist; he heard unspoken things. In the next instant, as she lay holding her breath, he had produced one of those lightning changes that left her so shaken, again slipping from beneath the covers without anger or abruptness to stand beside the bed, and again look down at her.

"Good night," he said agreeably, and waited a moment. When she made no reply he went out, closing the door behind him with unnerving gentleness.

She rang early enough next morning to catch Maggie at the flat.

"Maggie," she said without preamble, "I want a solicitor."

The line, unresponding, oddly seemed to her not so much empty as overfull.

"A rather . . . special kind, I expect," she fumbled, to this close-packed silence. "Someone very good for divorces."

"Mh'm," said Maggie after a moment. Her tone was devoid of satisfaction or *I-told-you-so,* carefully devoid even of too much comprehension. "Straightaway I can't tell you, I've not had much divorce business to give lawyers." She chuckled grimly, without amusement. "But I know where I can ask. Soon as I find out, I'll let you know." She rang off abruptly.

Passing by direction beneath the dark archway elbowed by two shops, Auriol entered an area of quiet; paved vistas, the giant rondure of the church, a handsome stone arcade, plain many-windowed structures not later than the eighteenth century: DR. JOHNSON'S BUILDINGS, announced one of their lintels. Even in this moment of qualms and apprehension, an indestructible element in her made her attempt to tear away the veil of two hundred years and see it as it must have been, with trees and grass, flowers and quiet paths and learned seclusion. Now the eye rested on courtyard expanses pitilessly stony; the Master's House with its garden was a slight solace, so was the well-fed white-and-ginger cat vocally in need of companionship, which she stroked with one finger through a mesh fence. Out of sheer nervousness she had come too early, and to sit for twenty minutes fidgeting in a waiting-room would be unbearable. Here to her right stood the great ancestor, its massive contours dominating all; the stony ghost eight hundred years old, the Temple itself. Auriol, born and living in London, had naturally never been in it. To kill time she went in now, passing into a vast lofty rectangle, then into the Round Nave, high and chill, smelling of ancient masonry and remote time and emptiness. There was a plain altar far away, there were pews in yellow wood for a sizable congregation, but they looked insignificant and utterly unrelated to the church itself; only one noble reredos measured up to this high barrenness that must once have been crowded with effigy burials blazing in red, blue, and gilt, with carved and canopied stalls for the Knights and chantry chapels of stone lacework, with Jerusalem itself present in the form of Crusaders' shields and gauntlets suspended here and there, all climaxed by the high altar and its masses, its pomp of vestments, processionals, incense, and music. And all but the shell of that towering, crowding mass of history wiped away; what time and neglect and Henry had left unmutilated, the Hun had reduced to dust and rubble, except fragments—an inscribed stone sealed away under thick glass, a couple of recessed tombs. Here in the circular emptiness where she stood, a few blackened effigies of Knights lay on the floor, uncomfortably reminiscent—with the wierd look of their crossed legs—of charred bodies snatched too late from a burning. Nearest her was a Templar with his face, his troubles, his very name, all rubbed away. She and her troubles would be similarly indistinct after five hundred years; the reflection seemed of little comfort. And as if in response to the thought, an unseen organist seated at an unseen organ pressed a single note, long sustained and dying away slowly, its melancholy invocation seeming to echo from some endless corridor of eternity.

Outside again, she saw her solicitor advancing to meet her, punctual to their appointment. A moment of cold misgiving overtook her as she reflected, all at once, that she had been less than completely frank with him, and wondered if her reservations and half-truths would affect the coming interview—for which, incidentally, she was paying fifty guineas.

The barrister was about sixty, she would judge; his hair was white, but he had retained plenty of it; his face was round and fresh-coloured, with neutral features and a neutral pleasant expression. What struck her chiefly was his eyes, blue, and of a candour and guilelessness almost childlike, which gave her a ridiculous feeling that it was somehow unsuitable to roil this pellucid simplicity with her troubled tale. He had responded charmingly to her solicitor's introduction, offering a chair and cigarettes and some general remarks on the weather, obviously to put her at her ease, a benevolent intention that failed of its effect. Her cicerone had seated himself slightly behind her and out of her range of vision, and rested there perfectly silent, but somehow the knowledge of this second presence was a constraint past all her expectation. It was all worse than she had imagined, and in a flash of prescience—acute if indistinct—she realized it was going to be still worse.

"Mr. Eliot has been good enough to communicate to me the details of your case," said Mr. Dysart, and smiled reassuringly. He touched some papers lying before him, the evasions and euphemisms she had dealt out to the solicitor, which were now handed on to the barrister. Naturally: and for the first time, with belated shock, there struck her an awareness of the destructive strain she had laid; the ever-magnified damage of the lie passed along a series of persons who depended on it as truth. How could such deception compare with the ordinary lie, its effect usually confined to the two persons between whom it had been spoken?

"You wish," his voice returned to her, as from across some intervening chasm, "to bring an action for divorce on grounds of cruelty. Mr. Eliot has informed you that this cruelty would have to be in the nature of physical maltreatment. You informed him that such, in your circumstances, is not the case—?"

He raised his eyes from the paper to lift an enquiring eyebrow at her; she nodded dumbly.

"Your husband's cruelty," he pursued, "seems to be of the nature that constantly creates, about you, an atmosphere of derision, frustration; an impossibility of reasonable communication; all of which affects you as nervous strain—severe and continual nervous attrition?"

She nodded again.

"Mr. Eliot has also told you," he resumed, "that cruelty of this nature—non-physical—is not grounds for divorce, until the marriage is of three years' duration?"

"He has," she responded, "told me that."

"And this being the case, he has told you," the inquisition continued, "that our only hope is to petition the courts for special permission to bring suit on the grounds of this—ah—minor cruelty? for which you must offer a physician's certificate that this mode of life is affecting your health? And," he emphasized, as if gathering it all up together and throwing it at her, "that such petition to plead on these special grounds may well, in the final event, be refused?"

"Yes," she articulated through dry lips. "He's told me all that."

"And nevertheless"—the shrug that he denied his shoulders was in his voice—"you have desired this consultation, as a means of—ah—exploring other avenues of action? to see whether there is not, after all, some alternative grounds on which you could sue for divorce?"

"Yes," she said. Her repeated assents sounded, in her own ear, incredibly dull and witless. "Yes, that's right."

"In that case," he remarked, "I do not like to suggest that you have thrown away a sizable number of guineas, but I fear I can tell you nothing that Mr. Eliot has not already told you." He pushed the papers slightly away, and turned to face her more fully. As he did so, something about his manner of performing the action struck her—as if, for all its implicit finality, it were somehow not final. The impression seized and let her go in the same instant, and meanwhile he was imparting his expensive wisdom.

"Let us take the various grounds of divorce which are entertained by the courts of this country." His blue eyes were affable and innocent. "For example, desertion: it must be for a three-year period, and after that time, if the deserted spouse will not sue, the deserting one is still held by the marriage. Cruelty: for actual brutality an action may be brought after one year of marriage, but for other cruelty such as in your case, not till after three years of marriage. Gross neglect, which sometimes includes evidence that the wife must support the husband: also not applicable in your circumstances. Adultery: the courts will wish to know where, and with whom, the acts of adultery took place, and will require corroborative evidence. Adultery is strong grounds, very strong grounds. Except that in your case, no such element enters into the situation—?"

"Nothing like that at all," she offered another of her dull concurrences.

"Very good." Again he had pushed her papers a little farther away, a gesture of increasing rejection. Yet in the same moment she felt it again, that indefinable, earlier impression of hers: the feeling that this apparent dismissal was prelude to some other, undisclosed intention. He had not finished with her, in spite of appearances; he was feeling his way. But to what, ultimately? One by one he had held up to her eyes the various instruments of divorce and had found in them nothing for her, no hope or prospect of hope . . . all at once she was aware of his guileless blue eyes upon her, and of the peculiar quality behind their guilelessness.

"Mrs. Hailes," he said abruptly, "are your intimate relations with your husband satisfactory?"

And here it was, the first blow: the first assault on the vulnerable place, that if continued must inevitably expose the hidden weakness. While still, considerably shaken, she groped for some means to parry or flee the mortal thrust—

"Are you," he was saying, "compatible sexually?"

From the way in which he waited, it was plain that he expected no ready answer; that his profession had inured him to these painful pauses from beings whose utmost privacies were under siege. When her silence had strung itself out, however, he resumed with a first accent of something else in his voice. Not of impatience— for it struck her now that this guileless-looking man was too vastly experienced for impatience—but of compassion.

"My dear Mrs. Hailes," he reasoned with her, "if you sue for divorce you may expect to be asked questions far more distressing than these, and in open court, before a particularly unsavoury section of gape-mouthed public. In such cases, we are down to the naked bedrock of humanity, like a surgeon at the operating-table; half-measures, with one or the other, are equally inadmissable. Therefore, if you expect to make the running, you must steel yourself. No one will spare you, nor must you hope to be spared. Now, had you rather terminate this interview, or may I proceed?"

"Please—please go on," she returned at once, and added clumsily, "I wasn't being missish, I was just— surprised."

Not *unnaturally*, conceded his smiling nod, as he said, "Since these shocks are unavoidable, better to be hardened to them in the privacy of an office. Are you," he repeated, "sexually compatible?"

"I—" she began, and stopped. Not till this moment had she realized how strong was her determination to avoid this aspect of the matter; to compel from the law a hearing for divorce on presentable, quotable grounds.

"Well no, not—not compatible," she continued guardedly, feeling for her next foothold, but he gave her no time.

"Well then, this incompatibility." He was gentle as always, but now she began to divine the degree of ruthlessness beneath it. "What is its nature?"

She made an indeterminate sound, now actively roused to clutch about herself some shreds of reticence; stripped of them she would feel ludicrous, exposed to the obscene laughter of an invisible audience. Worse than this, even, she felt the loop of his questions widening to include the person whom, in this particular aspect, she dreaded to betray.

"Is your husband responsible for this state of affairs?" he battered at her hesitation. "Has he ever refused intercourse?"

From pure shock she goggled at him, then mouthed, "Not—not exactly."

"Well then, you?" Only for the moment, she felt, did he by-pass the ambiguity of her answer; he would come back to it. "Have *you* ever refused intercourse, Mrs. Hailes?"

"No," she said quickly. "No, never."

"Well, in this case, since there is a mutual willingness, and yet at the same time you say there exists an incompatibility—just what is the nature of this incompatibility?"

And now she was impaled on the spear of his demand, on his first barb of impatience, and finally upon her own short-sighted tactics. Impossible to remain silent and equally impossible to answer, without admitting she had begun by lying.

"Is it merely physical, as for example some impediment, or disparity of proportion?" Still he tried to help her. "Or dissimilar sexual tempo? because such things can often be remedied by medical means and so forth. Or is the obstacle less material? is it spiritual, temperamental? Is it—"

"Oh Lord!" Badgered, she gave up all at once. "Actually, we've never been together as husband and wife, Never, since we were married," she asseverated with something like violence. "Not once."

"Well!" said Mr. Dysart forcibly. His eyes darted to a point behind her, and she felt, without seeing, the glance the solicitor gave him in return. "Well!" He leaned back with the air of a man who at last, after long delay, sights land. His next remark, equally emphatic, was in chorus with her solicitor's murmur, but both of them had said the same word. "A nullity!"

The atmosphere had changed, and obviously for the better. Yet her perception of this was less than her awareness of the man sitting behind her. By her misleading tactics, her incomplete confidences, she had placed him in this position—as taken in and hoodwinked, before the barrister he was supposed to be instructing; even with her back to him she could feel his resentment.

"This, my dear lady, puts a different complexion on things entirely," Mr. Dysart was saying with a new briskness, a new decision. "Well, since we've got so far forward—"

"It was stupid of me to hide it." Haltingly she tried to include both men in her apology. "But I'd so hoped for anything but those grounds, *anything*—"

"Quite," Mr. Dysart reclaimed her from her attempted amends. "Now from this point, I need ask you only a very few more questions. But I beg you, Mrs. Hailes: abandon circumlocution." His tone warned pointedly.

"Be explicit as possible, since upon your answers we will base our whole plea and contention, and by the quality of these answers of yours—their sincerity, their unassailability—your case will stand or fall."

She sat silent, rebuked; submissively waiting to hear more of this turn of events apparently propitious to her.

"Is your husband impotent?" he demanded next.

I don't know, hovered on the tip of her tongue, but it sounded too imbecile. "As far as I'm concerned," she amended, "he seems to be."

"Do you know what impotence means, in the male?" he shot at her. His eyebrows looked, at once, impatient and sceptical.

"I—I expect so," she stammered.

"It means," he continued pitilessly, "that there is no physical manifestation of desire, or no *effective* physical manifestation. Which of these, in your husband, seems to be the case?" As she hesitated, he warned, "I can put this question in another way, you know."

"Please don't," she said hastily, feeling that his concession to delicacy held a certain contempt for her. "So far as I know, I don't rouse him at all—in that way."

"In any other way?" His eyebrows arched another degree.

"No," she admitted. "Not at all."

"Are you responsible, in any manner," he pursued, "for this state of affairs? Have you ever created an atmosphere of derision, contempt, reluctance? anything which might considerably affect the powers of a sensitive man?"

"Never," she said firmly, and for the first time felt herself on unshakable ground. "I was prepared to be his wife in every sense of the word, I was ready to be—affectionate and—and responsive—and—" Too late she realized that all her effort to keep to the median and present a perfectly fair picture had not prevented him from seeing—and driving at—the weak place.

"Do you love your husband?" he asked.

"I liked him," she protested. "I wasn't in love with

him, but I liked him very much. I might have become very fond of him, if he hadn't mutilated—destroyed—everything between us."

"Well." He abandoned the point for another. "Is he elderly, or ill? do questions of health, or of some injury, enter into this situation—?"

"Nothing like that," she returned. "At least not that he's mentioned. He's only thirty-six and attractive, well built—perfectly strong and healthy. No, it's simply that when he's in bed with me, nothing happens—so far as I know."

"So far as you know?" He could not keep irony from his echo. "Aren't you sure?"

"No," she retorted angrily, and felt her cheeks burning. "If you want to know, he makes me so . . . timid, that I'm careful how I take any kind of liberty with him —very careful indeed."

Ah," he murmured on a soothing note. "But in view of this unhappy situation, your husband himself does not wish a divorce—?"

"He's never mentioned it," she shrugged. "And I haven't broached it yet. I shall," she assured him. "But how he'll react, honestly I don't know."

"Or might you," he pursued, "suggest to him the recourse of medical advice, as a possible solution—?"

"Ha!" she exploded, and abandoned herself; literally she felt the gates go down and the flood come sweeping through. "Offer him that sort of advice? You don't know him," she asseverated. "You don't know him. Either he'd take it as a piece of presumption or an intolerable insult, and he'd pretend not to understand, he'd look at me and smile and smile and ask what in the world I meant—you don't know his power of pretending nothing's wrong, you don't know. I haven't begun to convey it because I—I can't, he can make me wonder whether I'm on my head or my heels—or w-whether I'm the one, after all, that's off my rocker. And I'm not a hysterical type," she averred wildly. "No one's ever

70

doubted my sanity. But *I* doubt it, by the time he's through with me. And on top of everything——"

She had to refuel; it was quite a struggle to draw breath.

"——I can't do anything, I can't say anything, I can't have an idea or a friend that he doesn't——somehow—— *shame* it, make it rubbish. He makes *me* rubbish!" she blazed. "He can make me something that isn't, something that doesn't exist. And he enjoys it, you can see him enjoying it. And then you ask me"——aware that her voice had got away from her in an unpleasant degree, she could do nothing about it——"you ask me whether I've suggested his seeing a doctor! You don't know him!" she shrilled the refrain with climactic violence, as if it must illumine everything. "You don't *know* him!"

The silence held, for a long moment, only the sound of her breathing. If her outburst had aroused compassion in either man, Mr. Dysart at least gave no sign but to say, "That being the case, you are perhaps fortunate in having such valid and conclusive grounds for bringing suit." His mild voice was even milder, even more soothing. "We stand in a very strong position——with a nullity."

Only now did she seem to throw off the slowness and muzziness that had clogged her all these weeks and wake up to the thing she faced, inexorable.

"A nullity!" she echoed. The last shreds that dulled her understanding dissolved away, leaving a harsh glare. "That means a divorce suit on grounds of impotence——?"

"By no means." He was always gentle. "It means grounds of non-consummation of marriage, for such causes as may appear in the plea."

"No," she said at once. "I won't do that to him."

"But, my dear Mrs. Hailes——"

"I won't," she repeated. "It's horrible. It means he'd be asked those ghastly questions you asked me——in open court——"

"No, no," he demurred. "Nullity pleas are heard in camera."

"All the same." She shook her head violently, like a horse tormented by flies. "The people in chambers know. And he——he knows that they know."

"True," he murmured. "But unavoidable."

"Then——no. To pillory a man for that, it's the worst thing you could do to . . . and a man of m-my husband's type——no," she ended incoherently. "I won't. I can't."

Mr. Dysart's eyes had flickered, once again, in the solicitor's direction; she was uncertain whether he had shaken his head slightly, or not. Another silence followed, the silence of impasse.

"Do you mean to tell me," she flung into it, "that that's my only hope of divorce? There's no other way? none at all?"

"I have given you my poor opinion," he returned. Again, in his faultless demeanour, she felt the dismissal that he refrained from uttering. In this room, histrionics such as hers were an old story, which impressed no one and changed nothing. She felt the finality of his abandonment; behind her she heard the slight stir as the solicitor took up his briefcase and prepared to rise.

"Just——just one moment," she appealed desperately. "Let me understand my position."

Mr. Dysart bent his handsome white head, and the solicitor's slight movement ceased; in their mere listening was a sort of reprieve.

"Desertion must be for a period of three years," she began recapitulating. "So for me, desertion's out. And he doesn't knock me about, so cruelty's no good. And I won't sue on this other thing——this nullity——so that's no good either. And in any case"——she scanned the barrister's polite face, his air of listening not with interest but with forbearance——"since I've deserted him, it's he that must sue me. Is that right?"

Mr. Dysart nodded.

"And *that* means that if he won't move——if he won't take any action against me——then I can't get out of the marriage. And if I commit adultery and he refuses to sue me, it's the same again, isn't it?" her urgency pelted his impassiveness. "He can defeat me by merely sitting still and doing nothing. And if that's how he chooses to do it, this marriage could hold me forever. I'd have had it, wouldn't I? I'm trapped. Isn't that true?"

"Substantially, yes," he murmured.

"But you did say," she strove on, against her knowledge that she was overlapping her allotted time by sufferance, "you did say there was such a thing as special permission to sue, after only a year of marriage—"

Only a year, a sardonic echo brushed her ear.

"—on grounds of this other kind of cruelty, my husband's kind—this continuous harassment, belittlement, whatever you call it—"

"Assuredly we could petition for the privilege of suing," nodded Mr. Dysart, "provided you supplied us with a physician's statement that your health is seriously affected."

"I could get that without—without much difficulty, I expect. It'd be no lie, God knows." Feverishly she quested his inexpressive calm, his placid blue eyes, for some sign in her favour or against. "Well, then, will you? petition on my behalf to sue on this—this non-physical cruelty? Will you do that?"

A silence stretched out in the room, a considerable pause. At the end of it Mr. Dysart said, "Assuredly we will do that, if such are your instructions. But allow me to point out the inconsistency of following such a procedure—of pinning your hopes upon anything so uncertain—when you have within your hands the strongest material of all, a nullity." His voice, quiet and measured, held the remorseless tolling of a logic beyond argument or supplication. "The petition to sue after only a year of marriage, on these modified grounds, may be refused; whereas with a plea of nullity we can sue at once, as well as entering the arena with the most powerful weapons that can well be. So powerful, in fact, that aside from the distress of the hearing itself—which is, alas, inescapable—we need have little doubt as to the outcome. Or, all human affairs being uncertain," he qualified judicially, "as little as you like." It was he, this time, who scanned her face for signs of response. "It seems to me, in your special circumstances, that you are fortunate to have so valid a plea as nullity."

He stopped on a—for him—uncharacteristic note, doubtfully assertive; nor had his professional acumen misled him. And Auriol herself, sitting exposed to the slings and arrows of expert opinion, implacable, felt with surprise how able she was to withstand them; how, at each succeeding word of his, she hardened instead of weakened.

"All that may be true," she said with a composure that matched his own. "But the fact remains that I will not sue on those grounds. I refuse to consider it."

Mr. Dysart preserved an eloquent wordlessness; at the end of it, a shrug got away from him. "Pity," he disapproved, in a final rear-guard action. "To limit your counsel to the least effective procedure." He shrugged again, and she had an unnerving knowledge that her obstinacy alienated him and that not only his interest was withdrawn from her, but even his professional sympathy. So sharp was the impression that she ejaculated, suddenly fearful, "You mean you'd rather not take my case—except on grounds of nullity?"

"By no means," he returned. "I do not say that. But for my sins"—he was deprecating—"I am considered a sort of specialist in nullities. A specialist is always a little piqued"—his deprecation was now whimsical—"to be uprooted from the area of his specialty."

For a moment, too stunned even to think, she sat aghast before the percipience by which Maggie—to whom she had confided no word or detail of her trouble —had sent her not just to any lawyer, but to this particular sort of lawyer.

"By all means, then," he was saying. "You prefer us to chance the petition. If these are irrevocably your instructions, we shall move immediately on receipt of your physician's certificate." He paused. "But before resting finally on this decision, my dear lady, let us just once more, if you allow it, explore the grounds on which you oppose a nullity." Unexpected words, in a tone eminently reasonable, and once again she had a perception of his immense experience and skill, along with something else: a startled awareness of the new trail to which he had applied his sensitive nose, and of how futile her attempts would be to conceal anything from a man like this.

"I would not so press you," he was explaining apologetically, "but for my own impression that you desire a clear-cut divorce?"

"Yes," she said fervently. "Oh yes."

"Then I believe it my duty to try, at least, to wean you from your refusal of these best and most direct means, and—incidentally—from the dubious course to which you insist on committing us."

He held her eyes with his; paradoxically she felt herself impaled, harpoon-like, on their gentleness.

"Is it delicacy?" he pursued. "Delicacy alone, for yourself or your husband? But is not this somewhat jejune and immature, in these days when everything is said and everything is printed? Or it is the prospect of the hearing itself? Or has your aversion to being examined and certified as *virgo intacta* anything to do with—"

"Oh Lord!" Sudden harsh amusement emboldened her interruption and freed her tongue. "Who's *virgo intacta* nowadays? Or not many people of my age, I shouldn't expect. I'm almost thirty, Mr. Dysart. I was in love with a man that I expected to marry, and of course we lived together, what d'you think?" It was almost pleasant to be asserting herself for a change, instead of sitting humbly and being lectured. "That was almost three years ago and I haven't had a man since, but I'm certainly not a virgin. We were in love," she blurted needlessly, her voice dying to nothing. The room had vanished; for a moment her face, remote, was tranced with memory.

"Is it possible"—Mr. Dysart was alert, his lethal attention snagged on something new—"that this previous experience of yours might have been a factor in your husband's failure to consummate the marriage?"

"I shouldn't think so," she retorted, her unconstraint now well established; people got hardened to anything. "Matters never got far enough for him to find out, one way or the other. And even if they had," she pursued boldly, "he'd never have expected in a woman of my age what he might expect in a young girl—he's not that impractical."

"I see." Urbanely Mr. Dysart overlooked her excess of earthiness. "Well, now, Mrs. Hailes, suppose that your application to sue on special grounds is not successful; that from this process, you have got nothing. If your petition is refused, what then?" His eyes had renewed their hold on her; by now she found their guilelessness completely unnerving. "Also your husband, from what I gather, sounds to me like a man to be vigourously attacked, not approached with half-way measures. Against such a person one employs the heaviest possible weapon, not the lightest." He surveyed her again with that alarming quality which she had taken for innocence. "I must tell you, madam—"

Madam; she acknowledged with a wry inward smile this demotion from *my dear lady*, this new milestone in her progressive loss of favour.

"—that if squeamishness or delicacy, as I said, is your chief argument for opposing a plea of nullity, I for one do not find it sufficiently valid."

And again she was concerned: constrained to an avowal which she had had every intention of keeping from this mild-eyed man.

"Delicacy has nothing to do with it," she returned, her tone as measured as his own. "To tell you the truth, I'm . . . afraid."

On the last word, there fell a slight pause; a silence

76

with a quality of surprise in it, as if it sounded strangely in that room.

"A suit on grounds like that," she laboured on, "it's the best way you could stir up any man to retaliation, I should expect—to reprisal. And with a man of my husband's type"—she swallowed—"the possibilities are so unlimited that I don't like to think of them." She met his gaze, her mouth unsteady and her eyes large and fearful. "Just how he might try to get back at me, I don't know. And call me a coward, but I simply don't want to find out."

"My dear Mrs. Hailes!" The barristerial voice and eyebrows were slightly raised. "Are you suggesting—"

"Oh, no, no." She laughed shakily. "He'd never do anything violent. But he's so peculiarly . . . inventive . . . in making you realize his resentments, that I don't want to stir him up. I want," she qualified, with a wretched smile, "to walk around him as softly as possible."

A total silence fell; his look was withdrawn and speculative. When it returned upon her she realized that not only had she regained lost ground but that he was concerned for her personally, above and beyond the professional concern that he placed at the service of any client; the knowledge leavened her fears with a faint warmth.

"I see," Mr. Dysart responded warmly. "Then by all means, Mrs. Hailes, we shall enter our petition." He prepared to rise, and behind her, subconsciously, she heard the solicitor's similar movement. "I cannot tell you precisely how long this may take, but we will be in touch with you as soon as possible."

Half out of her chair, she was impaled all at once by a new daunting shaft of uncertainty.

"Mr. Dysart," she supplicated, "if I sue, and my husband defends—what then?"

"What then?" The question, like a hand, pressed him back into his seat. "Your husband is well-off, I gather?"

"Very well-off."

"In that case, having the means to exhaust every device of obstruction, he may keep the case from coming to trial for a year. No more," he assured her, a form of comfort as solacing as a bludgeon. "And once we have him in court, it all depends on which of you impress the court as having spoken truth. I myself"—he smiled at her, and his smile was entirely charming—"do not anticipate any difficulty on that score."

"And just one more question." So many postscripts and afterthoughts, how did one think of everything . . . "In a suit for nullity—could he defend?"

"Defend a nullity? unusual, but not unknown." His reflective gaze scanned cryptic legal horizons. "But in your case, where there has been no reluctance—"

"No," she interrupted forcibly. "No."

"—and since you have not suffered this unnatural mode of life in silence, but have been driven by it to seek divorce—I somehow do not believe that your husband will defend. But if he does, I am not unduly disturbed by the prospect." His eyes gleamed suddenly paler as from a glancing ray of light, and she understood how much he would enjoy pulverizing Ivor, though his immaculate professionalism forbade him to say so.

Outside the chambers the solicitor's farewells were polite but icy. She walked out of the Temple in the realization that her sin—her failure to confide in him honestly and completely—was unforgiven.

7

The physician's certificate presented no difficulty; her mother's doctor was an old family friend, thank heaven there would be no complication about that, at least . . .

Walking steadily, unseeing and absorbed, she emerged all at once from this thought to find herself at a certain point in the Strand. It was this point, merely geographical, that all at once pushed her into doing what she had had no previous thought of doing. Just across the road was the book trade's warren of Bedford Street, where stood Stormonth's august portals; passing through them, she thought as usual that only a publisher so massively traditional and so massively solvent could afford an entrance so shabby.

Here, the outcry of welcome surprised her. She had imagined herself applying for any overflow of work they might give her now and again; in actual fact she was petitioned, practically on bended knee, to take back her old job again.

"No one to touch you since you left," puffed her superior, more dangerously stout than ever. "Not since you foully betrayed us, you baggage. Roly, love"—he actually sat up straight with a gigantic wheeze, token of effort—"all's forgiven, for Christ's sake come back. That journeyman's she-ass I hired in your place is hopelessly bogged down, she's lost. Four books behind, and a couple of them conceivably important—she can't cope, that's all. She's got her Firsts and she knows her facts, but she doesn't begin to have your sense of period, your gift for *instantly* getting the quality of a book—"

"Dear, dear." She laughed on a note unheard by her in months. Already the working idiom, ribald and sometimes foul-mouthed, was reviving her like the open air after entombment. "If I'd known I was that wonderful, I'd have squeezed you for more money."

"And if *I'd* known what was going to happen," he retorted, "I'd have poisoned your intended. How is he by the way, your husband?"

"Very well, thanks." She smiled inwardly at the blatant uninterest of the question. "Only see here, Mark, I couldn't come for the whole day, not at first—"

Immovably, doggedly, she resisted the volume of his importunities.

"No, no, not at first," she kept saying. "I couldn't, Mark, honestly I couldn't. Eleven to three," she repeated her first offer. "Every day from eleven to three, and I won't lunch—it's the way we'll have to do it just now. You see," she was forced to appeal, "I don't want my—I don't want Ivor to know."

His bombardment was suddenly silenced; he gave her a look, sharply speculative, then carefully neutral.

"Well, if you say." His grunt was ill-contented. "You're the one that knows how much time you can give us, I reckon. Well, small mercies and so forth." He entered upon the first labour of rising. "Come along, Roly, I'll take you on a triumphal tour."

"Not now," she fended him off. "We'll arrange things, I'll be in touch with you. Tell me, how's everyone? Tom, and everyone?"

"Oh, splendid, splendid. Tom's as usual, you know Tom—same old battle-axe and welkin-ringer." His expression changed. "Marriage agrees with you, I must say—you're quite overpowering. *Mmmmmm!*" his nostrils flared in burlesque appreciation of her perfume, his eyes canvassed her expensive elegance up and down. "Leisure, my God, no denying it, it puts a high varnish on people." He chuckled maliciously. "A little honest work'd knock off your gloss in two two's, I promise you."

"I shouldn't mind," she assured him.

"Quite lovely," his glance continued to rake her, stem and stern. "A little jaded with marital disport and high living, perhaps, but lovely."

Oh my God, she thought, as she smiled and petitioned again, "But please, Mark, my coming back—don't broadcast it, *please*."

"I'll certainly keep my mouth shut," he promised after a moment. "But I can't go about swearing people to secrecy, can I?" He frowned. "Still, your husband's nothing to do with publishing—I don't expect there's any special reason he'd find out."

He found out, naturally. It took a little longer than she would have expected, but he found out. On this evening when they had stayed home, with a lifeless rain seeping and trickling outside, she was reading, and looked up once or twice to find him contemplating her. Aside from being meditative his air was unrevealing, yet in her experience these prolonged scrutinies always led to something. Each time, hastily lowering her eyes, she had waited with unease and a growing desire to burst out, *Why are you staring at me? what is it this time, for God's sake?* Actually she remained silent, rather than ask and invite his bland denials and disclaimers, his eel-like faculty for twisting out of anything he pleased.

"Don't you find it boring," he observed finally, "to get through the whole day by yourself?"

The question, for all its seeming unconcern, set up a tingling along her every instinct of wariness and alarm. "Oh, I don't know," she parried, playing for even a few seconds of time. "Not too boring, specially."

"Now that, I don't understand." He was judicial. "You're not as empty-headed as most women, you've had a profession. You're not the sort of fool that can spend hours before her mirror, plastering on muck and sorting out each individual eyelash. You're not a card-player, so you can't kill an afternoon that way. Tell me," he invited, on a note almost cooing, "what do you do with yourself? how do you, actually, spend your time?"

"Well," she began, "there's the house."

"*This* house? but none of the actual work here devolves on you, does it?"

"No." Hastily she conceded the perfections of Ivor's couple, Mr. and Mrs. Patcham, with whom she would not have dared interfere even had there been need; Ivor had seemed only too grateful that they would stay on in spite of the irruption, into this clockwork bachelor establishment, of a wife. "But still we do have people to dine, don't we, there's always a certain amount of organizing—and bills and things . . . and then," she digressed too rapidly, "I see Mummy a good bit. We drive to the country or go to films or theatres, I've never been able to do those things with her and she adores it. Or I lunch with someone I . . . things like that," she continued vaguely, and wondered why she put any hope or trust in the protective value of this vagueness. "And I've done other things I never had time for, like going to the V and A and the National Portrait, things like that."

"Useful, museums," he commented. "As a way of passing time."

"Yes," she agreed uncertainly; he was too affable.

"Also theatres and cinemas, of course. Then your work at Stormonth," he concluded negligently, almost dreamily. "You must find that useful too."

She took an instant to reckon herself with the fact of being taken red-handed, and another instant to make a heartening discovery; she was unmoved and slightly grim, not frightened or cowed, and if he expected her to be she was in for a disappointment. How he had found out touched her mind, but only for the fraction of a second. Whether by ferreting, by accident, or by guess—

one of his pounces confirmed by her own confusion—was unimportant. But in what degree this might be instrumental in bringing matters to a head, was extremely important.

"Your involved little traps," she retorted. "As you say, I'm not too good at killing time. Actually, it was driving me up the wall."

"And so," he picked up the thread, "you sneaked into your old job again—behind my back."

"Sneaked? if you like." Her coolness still surprised her; only now she realized to what extent that job had strengthened her and put firm ground under her feet. She could never have faced up to him like this when eaten hollow by idleness. "Whether I sneaked or not, isn't it irrelevant?"

"Irrelevant?"

"Yes. The relevant thing, it seems to me," she pursued with increasing boldness, "is that I did it your way at first. I stopped working because you wanted me to, I tried it your way. Well, it didn't work, for me. I can't face it any more—waking up in the morning and knowing there's a whole empty day before me. It's desperate, I can't any more. I can't, that's all."

"That was your reason." He nodded consideringly. "Was it?"

"Yes." She was boundlessly relieved that he seemed nothing worse than thoughtful. "And after all I—I've kept it to hours when you're not at home, anyway. Eleven to three, you're never here. And—and I'm not neglecting anything, you said yourself I'm not needed for . . . running the house—" she broke off, angry that —as so often in speaking with him—she had begun to stammer.

"No, you don't run the house," he concurred.

"No. So you see, if it doesn't affect you, you can't possibly object." She was uncomfortably breathless; his ascendancy over her was something, apparently, not to be dispelled in five minutes. "I had to have something to *do*. I didn't want to go on like that and—and run into some sort of—of breakdown."

"And that," he reaffirmed mildly, "was your reason for going back to Stormonth."

"Yes."

"Your only reason?"

She looked at him, genuinely uncomprehending yet aware of a smile that had begun to lurk in the corners of his mouth.

"Of course," she answered. "What other reason could there be?"

"Come, come," he murmured with a quizzical amusement that made her, all at once, long to strike him. "Let's not be childish, shall we?"

"What other reason could I have"—she was becoming a little strident—"for going back to Stormonth?"

"You'd like me to say it?"

"Yes!"

"But you see, my love," he purred dulcetly, "it happens that I'd like *you* to say it."

"Your nasty little hints," she flung at him, "that you won't come out with. It's cowardice, that's all, beastly poisonous cowardice."

"By all means," he returned negligently, his tone suggesting that he was no longer even interested. "As you like."

For another long moment she fought for breath, for self-control, and for recovery from her moment of boldness; never before had she addressed him with so near an approach to invective.

"You say I've some—some concealed reason—for going back to Stormonth," she tried again, with an unconscious accent of desperation. "But you won't say what it is."

"I thought we'd finished with the topic," he returned absently. "It's beginning to bore me."

Struck dumb once more, as rapidly as her agitation would permit she summed up the situation. With accustomed skill he had led the two of them into an entrapment of exchanges without beginning or end; a lunatic circle with no exit point. *Crazy, you're crazy*, was actually on her tongue, when an alarm bell from her deepest instinct stopped her dead; *mad, insane, crazy*, these were words that she would address to him at her peril. Instead, something else began bearing her up: a heartening wave of scorn, disgust, impatience. From its crest she head a voice say abruptly, "Ivor, let's divorce."

The words came back on her as improbable. She had not intended saying them this soon or like this, without careful preparation; simultaneously she felt the relief of the irrevocable.

"This is simply no good," she pursued. "It's no good at all living like this—going on like this. Let's divorce."

Some moments of silence passed, perhaps not many, but she felt them spreading out and out like a smooth, deep, unrevealing pool.

"Divorce," he murmured, after this blank. If her proposal had surprised or disturbed him in any way, there was absolutely no sign of it; such control was inhuman. "Fancy that. And all the time I'd thought we were going on so well together. A rude awakening, isn't it—from a dream of connubial bliss?"

At once she understood what she was in for; another of those desperate exhausting sessions of blank evasion, pretended incomprehension, laced with covert mockery. Nevertheless, and with all her resources, she braced herself to fight it. This encounter was not like any that had gone before; this one was crucial.

"I don't doubt that it's all my fault," she bore on doggedly. "I think I'm perfectly unsatisfactory to you in every way, and I don't see why you should put up with —with this kind of life. I'm only sorry I've turned out such a—a disappointment. I'm sorry I've been so inadequate." Strenuously taking the blame was perhaps the least fatal way to go about it, she thought, and plowed on, "Well, no one could expect you to go on and on like this, I know *I* don't expect you to. There's not very much in it for you—you can't be happy."

"I? but of course I'm happy." He was ingenuously wide-eyed. "I'm perfectly happy."

She had to take a long moment to draw breath; to reassemble herself against this mammoth perverseness.

"How can you be?" she argued. "How can you be happy, with so much between us that's . . . wrong?"

"Wrong?" He was more innocently puzzled than ever. "Is anything wrong?" As she sat dumbfounded before this, unparalleled even for him, he continued, "I thought we were leading an eminently civilized existence." A wave of his hand invoked as witness the gleaming, opulent room. "We don't quarrel, we don't bore each other, we get on better than a hundred married people I know. And you, my adored"—his glance flicked her—"you don't seem to scorn the embellishments, either."

She ignored the hit at her expensive clothes, part of a vague campaign to make herself alluring enough, exciting enough to overcome . . .

"Civilized, yes." Laboriously she hewed to the line. "Maybe civilization isn't enough."

"You've got your work." He shrugged. "You've gone back to your work."

"That isn't enough either," she countered boldly. Having thrown down the gauntlet, she would not be put off. "Anyway, you don't like my working. Sooner or later there'll be trouble about it, or if not that then something—something else—"

Nervous effort was disjointing her speech; by an effort of will she mastered it.

"—it's not one thing, or two things," she pursued. "It's everything. Everything's wrong."

His silence was total for a moment, but so was his composure. "Most of the couples I know," he observed negligently, "haven't slept together for years, but people don't seem to make your hot-blooded thing of it. Establishments aren't broken up for such reasons."

But they slept together at first, she retorted silently. *At some time of their lives, they did.* Not daring such naked pointedness, she cast about for something as little provocative as possible, but was forestalled.

"In any case," he was saying, "for this little *jeu* that you contemplate, there's such a thing as grounds. I haven't bashed you, you haven't slung the teapot at me, and so forth. We haven't deceived each other—or," he amended, "I can speak for myself, at least. So what do we offer in the way of grounds, you and I?"

On the verge of answering, she caught herself back. From her too-great promptness of reply he might infer the background presences of the solicitor, the barrister, the conferences—all of which she must conceal from him at all costs.

"I know you haven't bashed me, and I haven't picked up the fire-irons," she began, with wariest caution masked behind a semblance of humour. "And I've not committed adultery, any more than you—"

He murmured something; at a guess she made it out, *Charmed to hear it.*

"But I believe there's a—a sort of technical cruelty that's accepted as grounds. I mean, where there's no question of physical violence, just friction and nervous strain, and if you can get a doctor to certify that it's affecting your health"—fearful of betraying her perilous state of legal enlightenment, she hesitated again—"you can sue for divorce on—on that."

"Sue for divorce on nothing more than minor disruptions?" He was sceptical and amused, equally. "In English law? Where did you hear of any such thing?"

"I—I don't know. I heard of it—somewhere."

"And don't remember where? it's a fairly striking bit of information." His eyes held hers with sudden intensity. "Who told you that?"

"No one *told* me, it's an impression." Near to panicking, she held tightly to her casual unshaken tone. "Or something I've known for so long, and so vaguely—"

"A vague impression, my love, is not much basis for divorce."

"No, but I *did* hear it," she struggled on. "And from a knowledgeable source. I've an impression of that too. One of Stormonth's solicitors maybe . . . ?" With precipitate gratitude she latched onto an inspiration so sound and plausible. "Yes, that was it, *now* I remember! And I even remember his saying"—emboldened, she plunged on—"that they were very special grounds and you had to petition to sue on them, but that permission was sometimes given. He talked as if suits like that"—she had to draw a long nervous breath—"he said they were by no means unknown."

"Why would a publisher's lawyer," he queried blandly, "be discoursing at such length on divorce?"

"It must have had something to do with a book. Perhaps there was some possibility of libel, or something." She embroidered more boldly as she felt herself on firmer ground. "Where there's any question like that, we always take expert advice—legal opinion."

"And have you," he suggested, "been following your employer's example?"

As she stared at him, caught unawares in her moment of premature relief, he was saying, "Have you also been taking legal advice—expert opinion?"

"No," she lied uncompromisingly.

"You're sure? all this forensic fluency isn't the result of consulting solicitors, barristers—?"

"I wouldn't have, not till we'd talked." The least hint of wavering would push her down the sheer glassy plunge on whose edge she had been performing her egg-dance. "I'd rather *you* consulted them, if it came to that."

"Well, if you haven't been closeted with Q.C.'s and what-not"—he chose to ignore her last remark—"I can only regard you, admiringly, as a born Portia."

"I'm no Portia." With carefullest patience she by-passed his ironic applause. "It's simply that I rememberer it at random—about there being this special kind of suit. We—I mean—one could find out."

"Assuredly one could find out," he concurred. "Without too much difficulty, I expect."

"Yes." Too eagerly she ran to meet this concurrence. "And you see that if there *is* such a way of suing, it's certainly better than adultery or brutality or—or horridness like that."

"Yes." He nodded again. "Compared with that sort of thing, this special plea would seem a more or less simple approach to the problem."

"You see—?" A vertigo of hope took her; she had not expected it to be so easy. "Ivor, you do see that, don't you?"

"Simple, yes, and quite civilized." Thoughtfully weighing it, he nodded. "Yes. In the archaic state of our divorce laws, I see that this—ah—technical cruelty caper is much the best way out."

"Will you then?" She was still a little light-headed with the comparative ease of her victory. "Will you, Ivor?"

"Will I?" he echoed, with the slight irritation of one recalled from a relevant to an irrelevant issue. "Will I what?"

"What?" she repeated, incredulous. "Will you let us divorce?"

"You and I? divorce?"

"Ivor," she appealed, on a first strident note. "Don't drive me mad merely for the fun of it. What else have we been talking about, for God's sake? What were *you* talking about, just now?"

"Oh, that? mere hypothesis—academic." He was negligent. "I certainly wasn't discussing it as having any application to us."

"Then you won't let us?" Her voice came back to her breathless and faint. "Divorce?"

"Of course not," he returned. "Don't be silly."

A pause opened between them like a cleft split by an axe; caught in it she sat, stupidly surprised that she was appalled; that he could still appall her. He could not be pinned to a direct answer about anything, by any person, compulsion, or set of circumstances. And far from decrying this horrid accomplishment, that made dirt of the human assumption that one reasonable intelligence is accessible to another, he took pride in it. The knowledge goaded her into one, solitary grim intent. She would not be defeated by this distortion in him, she would not be deflected or silenced. At the same time there was little reassurance in feeling that her hold on her self-control was slipping away.

"Tell me then," she challenged, in no conciliatory voice. The hiatus, which had seemed endless, had probably lasted a minute or so. "What *did* you think about us? How did you picture our life together, year after year? What was your idea about—about how we'd go on?"

"I'd never given it any particular thought—the need of it never occurred to me, actually." While she registered his effrontery in assuming that she would be satisfied forever with such a mode of existence, he continued, "I took for granted we'd go on like other married couples. Be together. And sometime later, perhaps—"

If he hesitated, it was all but imperceptible.

"—have a family," he continued. "Have children."

She burst out laughing. The sound, harsh and deep, offended her own ears. She laughed on and on, unable to stop; all in the same instant afraid of its effect on him, and of her own inability to explain that it held no mockery, no derision, only purest despair.

"Sorry," she struggled against it, herself disintegrated by the wounding merriment, "sorry, I—I wasn't laughing at you, I only—I—"

Calm, attentive—this attentiveness upset her most of all—he waited till she had controlled herself and wiped the tears from her eyes.

"You're my wife, as it happens," he said, immovable as if the room had not barely ceased echoing to the horrid cachinnation. "This is our home. Here we are and here we'll stop, so far as I'm concerned. We've not begun suit for divorce, and we're not going to divorce."

"Oh, no?" she lashed out with sudden rage, almost hearing her every instinct of civilization snap apart viciously, like violin strings. "Who says so? You? or I?"

"Don't shout, if it's not asking too much." The unaltered quiet of his voice, almost murmurous, rebuked her stridency. "You see, my love, I understand you all too well." His triangular smile was slight but baleful. "You, and the reasons behind your actions—all pitiably transparent." He smiled again. "Your return to Stormonth for the sake of resuming your affair with that pair of shoulders, that M'Kell—"

She gaped at him.

"That's—" With her stupefaction mingled a surprise that after a year or more, after one glimpse of Tom and a few words with him, Ivor should remember his name. "That's utterly—fantastic," she managed, and stopped again.

"Why? 'Roly,' " he quoted. "His repellent pet name for you. Very matey indeed."

"That's idiotic," she blurted. "Everyone called me Roly."

"Not with that inflection, my sweet. I happen to be," he pointed out, "extremely good at inflections."

"Not this time," she gainsaid, wishing it were a devastating retort instead of a lame one. "You couldn't be further off the mark."

"Now come," he urged affably. "You were sleeping with him at the time we met, weren't you? Or you had done, not too long before."

"Tom, of all—why, I've never even had a date with him—" She abandoned protest and assumed the offensive. "Anyway, if you thought I was sleeping with him, why'd you have anything to do with me? Or no," she changed course violently, before he could reply. "It's too"—again, at its source, she checked *crazy*—"it's too preposterous." The heat of anger was all over her body, making her feel unclean and eroding her power of self-defence. By contrast, in her husband's cool ascendancy, she could see his relish in her struggles, her trembling voice and trembling body. "I won't talk about it. I won't!"

"Let's not," he agreed pleasantly. "It's a minor matter, isn't it, compared to this other inspiration of yours —this divorce? And I know what's behind that. Or rather," he qualified, his voice suddenly different, "who."

As she goggled at him, more than ever bewildered—

"It's not your own idea, you know," he was continuing. "It's been put into your head by someone else."

"Will you kindly tell me," she managed with difficulty, "just what you're talking about?"

He shrugged, smiling again. "You *are* a bit soft, my love." His inflection was kind and understanding. "Not your fault, of course, that you take impressions too easily. From the very outset I could see that she'd an unhealthy influence over you."

"Why, you . . . you're crazy." The forbidden word was out, in spite of her; she was recklessly indifferent, even as she saw the passing balefulness in his face. "You mean that Maggie's anything to do with me wanting a divorce? Maggie, of all people?" She had regained some power of self-defence. "Why, I've not even seen her for months. I was ashamed to, after the rotten time you gave her here."

He seemed to consider a moment, calmly, then said all at once, "You've been in touch with her over this."

"I haven't," she returned, a second too late.

"There, you see? You admit it."

"I don't admit it. I don't." In the midst of her violence she realized her hesitation, and how fatal it would be to any assertion of hers thereafter. Moreover, swarming fears and conjectures eroded her. That call of hers to Maggie for a solicitor, had he somehow overheard it? In this moment of demolishment, she could not remember. "I've admitted nothing of the sort," she persisted with a sort of desperation.

"You're a poor liar," he compassionated, as if she had not spoken. His capacity for pouncing, by guesswork, had done him good service; his clairvoyance which once she had thought of as a unison of both their spirits, now appeared to her malign. "Obviously you can't deny it. And that being the case, I fear that your friend's asked for it."

"Asked for—for what?" she gasped.

"For whatever may follow, naturally." His tone was more and more negligent. "Is she such a fool that she doesn't realize she's exactly as vulnerable as anyone else in the theatrical profession? What good does she think she does herself, inviting a lawsuit and giving me a wide choice of grounds? Alienation of affections, conspiracy, undue influence? Complete"—he added smilingly—"with the implications and undercurrents that her appearance confirms in advance. Do her good? It'll ruin her."

"You . . . " She must suffocate, she thought, or something must give way in her head. "She's—she's done *nothing*—none of what you say. She's never done anything to you."

"She needn't *do*," he explained, delicately touching the verb with emphasis. "For me, she need only be."

"You couldn't"—she strove wildly, against his pleasure in his turn of phrase—"do such an injury—risk doing it to a person that's—that's never—you couldn't."

"No?" he murmured. "Couldn't I?"

"Damn you!" she bayed at him, her voice suddenly unrecognizable, more an animal's howl than human. "Damn you, damn you, damn you!"

8

As soon as Maggie had handed back the menu and the wine-list with a conclusive gesture, with equal conclusiveness she faced around and demanded, "How are you?"

"All right," said Auriol. She wondered whether apprehension were shortening her breath. "I'm all right."

Maggie took time for a brief, suspicious stare before returning, "I suspect you're talking balls. Even," she qualified, "even though you look more or less all right."

"Do I?" asked Auriol spiritlessly. *How'll I tell her?* strove among her confused thoughts, like a swimmer floundering and failing. *I should've told her before she dragged me to this place. But over the phone, how could I?*

"You look all right and you should be all right," Maggie bludgeoned away. "You're in your proper job and your proper environment again, which should set you up no end. You're in a fair way to get shut of Ivor." She checked suddenly. "Or the divorce is going badly? Is that the trouble?"

"You're a bit previous." Auriol smiled with an effort. "It couldn't be good or bad, at this stage."

"But it's on?"

"Oh yes, they're—they're doing all that can be done, I expect. And I never thanked you for sending me to that solicitor," she added, awkward in awareness of this late acknowledgment. "He took me to a barrister who's wonderful, perfectly wonderful."

"You really think that? you've confidence in him?" Maggie demanded. "You're satisfied to have it in his hands?"

"Perfectly," Auriol acceded. "He's right for me, he's perfectly right."

"Well then, it's not the divorce that's worrying you," Maggie declared, and turned a dissatisfied eye on her companion. "Is it your mother, then?"

"Oh no. I mean," Auriol explained, "it's a shadow, yes, it's there, but it's just like Mummy—it doesn't ask to be noticed." The glottal twang, as she swallowed hard, was so manifestly painful that she herself looked surprised. "The truth is, she doesn't care any more about living."

"You can't help that," Maggie pointed out, subdued. "Does she know about the divorce?"

"Oh *no!* she mustn't." Auriol's voice and eyes quickened with alarm. "She lives wrapped up in dreams of my wedded bliss and being rich and happy forever." A grimness reinforced her emphases. "She mustn't be upset and she won't be—not if I've anything to say about it."

"But your telephone being changed, what about that?"

"I gave her some excuse—it was easy, the phone system being the shambles it is."

"M'hm. Well"—Maggie renewed the attack—"if it's not the divorce that's on your mind, and not your mother, what is it?"

Maggie, Auriol had almost blurted, when a hand and arm appeared in front of her, depositing the first course in its silver holder banked with ice. Another hand was pouring the first crystalline drops of the accompanying Montrachet into Maggie's glass; Auriol, abjectly grateful for reprieve if only by postponement, watched her taste and consider them—no empty ritual, for Maggie

95

really knew about wine. "A tiny bit young maybe," she said at last, "but not too bad." She contemplated the rosy opulence of her lobster cocktail. "God, isn't that beautiful! And I'm starving."

Perforce, Auriol picked up her fork. In this setting of festive food and drink, of tables scintillant with snow, silver, and flowers, with the gay restaurant hubbub all about, how taint the moment with her poisonous communication that must change it all to dust and ashes, to bitterness and anxiety?

"Really good food they've got here," said Maggie, tucking in with zest. "One of the really durable pleasures, after everything else's let you down." She glanced at Auriol's serving. "Isn't it all right?"

"It's wonderful."

"Then why aren't you eating?"

Auriol protested, "I am," an untruth so palpable that Maggie disdained to contradict it, and finished her own cocktail with a slight frown and noticeably less enthusiasm. When the servers were being removed she demanded without preamble, "Is it money?"

"Money?" Auriol echoed blankly, left behind by the digression.

"That's worrying you?"

"Oh no. That is, it's not worrying me." Grateful again to be distracted from the gnawing dread, Auriol considered. "From the beginning I knew I'd have to have a reserve, and it's just a question of getting it together—saving every penny I can. These things move slowly, you know—when I need my bit of money I'll have it, more or less."

"Promise," said Maggie abruptly, "to let me make up whatever you need and haven't got, for this caper. Give it to you, I mean. Or lend it to you, if your pride and so forth."

"Oh Maggie!" The gratitude that flooded her was no less prompt than her refusal. "My angel Maggie, I couldn't. Thank you a thousand times, but I couldn't possibly."

96

"And for Christ's sake why not?"

"Because I haven't the faintest idea what it'll cost. I couldn't let you in for an unpredictable expense, and I couldn't let myself in for an unpredictable obligation. No." Decisively she fended off the other's attempt to speak. "Thank you from my heart, but no. And please, please, Maggie, don't bring it up again." She lowered her voice, for again they were being served. "Ever."

Maggie shrugged and turned her attention to a sumptuous concoction of veal folded upon ham, garnished with truffles and asparagus and masked with a velvety sauce. Plying her knife and fork with somewhat diminished zest, she scowled; that Auriol took the scowl for annoyance or resentment was only a proof that she knew Maggie less well than she imagined.

"Food *is* a consolation, I don't care what you say," Maggie declared with a zest somehow childlike, as if someone had contradicted her. She glanced at Auriol's serving, hardly diminished by the slivers cut from it, and forbore to comment, only remarking instead, "There's a friend of yours over there."

"Where? I don't see . . . Oh yes, imagine! Tom." A shadowy amusement touched her for a moment. "D'you know, this is the first time I've seen him at large, away from Stormonth, I mean? And *the* girl with him." On the edges of her smile hovered an old hurt. "So that's what she's like."

"Savage-tempered," Maggie diagnosed off-handedly. "Conceited. And ruthless? God."

"She's a lovely piece." Across the bright restaurant Auriol stared at the nymph in shining almond-green satin, the flawless throat and shoulders, the piquant face. "How can Tom afford to bring her to a place like this?"

"He can't—got it in one. Unless," Maggie supplemented, "he's got a private till somewhere."

"No, he's got nothing like that. We're good friends, very good friends, and he's always told me all about himself, quite openly," Auriol gainsaid. "He's such a confiding, easy-going old thing."

"That's his trouble," Maggie grunted. She scoured her plate with a piece of bread, as if in pointed rebuke to Auriol's laggard appetite. "A little stiffening would make another person of him."

"He's all right," Auriol murmured. Her half-smiling, half-remote look was still on the couple. He's in love."

"Yes, poor bastard—I wish him joy of her. Just coffee, black," she threw at the waiter, paused till their table was cleared, then demanded abruptly, "Do you miss him?"

"Who, Tom?" At once she laughed at her failure to keep pace with the kangaroo-leaps of Maggie's thought. "Good heavens, *no*, of course I don't miss Ivor. I dread the very thought of him."

"And I shouldn't expect"—Maggie was hesitant for once—"that you miss the luxury, the atmosphere of money, the things you could buy?"

"How can you think so?" Auriol's vigour of rebuttal, her first that evening, was as if a nerve had been touched. "I don't want any part of it—of anything that's *him*." Sickeningly, on the heels of her vitriolic emphasis, came the reminder of what had not been said and what must be said, whose every postponement thrust her deeper into the pit of apprehension. *Now, now,* clamoured an inward voice. At all costs, whether Ivor would or would not implement his atrocious threat, Maggie must be warned, alerted. *Now!* shrilled the silent voice, again, and for a pin-point of time she knew the semi-swoon and cold sweat of cowardice . . . Too late; cups had been placed on the table, the black steaming liquid was being poured. A plate of beruffled *friandises* accompanied it, Cape gooseberries in delicate white frosting and the like.

"Lovely coffee," said Maggie, sipping. "Ouch! I'm seared north to south. Tell me"—her accent of determination was back in force—"are you glad you've your job again? Are you glad you're working?"

"How can you ask?" Harried from her preoccupation, Auriol answered with shaky violence. "The release, you can't think! Like—like escaping from death."

"Precisely." With deliberation, Maggie put down her coffee-cup; her measured tone served notice to her companion that the moment was upon her. She should have known that Maggie hung on like a bulldog, never letting anything go unfinished, a quality that was one source of her considerable professional success.

"All right," she was saying, "it's not the divorce that's worrying you, and it's not your mother. You aren't hankering after Ivor, and you're happy with your job. If it's none of these things, what is it?"

"It's me." Auriol scurried behind a last, craven lie. *Not now, I can't tell her now and spoil everything,* she thought frantically. *I'll write—I'll write her tomorrow.* "You shouldn't have dragged me out, that's all. I'm not fit company for man or beast—I told you."

"I'd be obliged if you didn't talk balls. At least, not to me," returned Maggie. "You're upset and badly upset, if I know anything about you. So"—her level tone, her extorting eye, held the quarry on a final impalement— "if it's none of those other things, what the hell's eating you?"

"Maggie," Auriol appealed all at once, abandoning her straw defences; her voice had the fainting note of extremity. "Please don't be—I mean, I couldn't help— it was such a shock, so—unthinkable—" she paused and forced coherence on her broken gabbling. "Ivor said that you were responsible for my wanting a divorce, that you—you'd influenced me. He said—he said he'd—he'd sue you." It was out; she paused in a shrinking terror, as if awaiting the detonation of a grenade she had thrown. When only silence happened she ventured a furtive glance not at but toward Maggie, lacking courage to look straight at her, and waited.

"I knew it," were Maggie's first words. She replaced her cup in the saucer with a collected gesture. "I always knew it." Her tone was so evidently of soliloquy that

Auriol, daring to offer no word, hazarded a second glance and again waited.

"I knew it'd destroy me one day," went on the strange self-communion. "This God-damned shell that was foisted on me, and that I can't do anything about." Her glance and tone returned to Auriol. "You see what'll happen, don't you, with my type—my looks? The implications of such a suit, the undercurrents—don't you see them?"

"I don't expect he'll do it," Auriol besought. "I had to tell you, but I don't think he'll really do it."

"You don't?" Maggie was sardonic. "I read him differently."

Protestation rose to Auriol's lips and died at birth, too poor and sickly to survive; she could now risk a sustained glance at the other woman in her stony abstraction—the abstraction with which one contemplates catastrophe. Maggie's face was grey, sponged of expression; her eyes were remote.

"And in my profession, too," she continued in that frozen clam of prophecy. "He can destroy me. I can fight back, I can even win, but all the same I'll be done for. In this charming world, you never get clean again from that kind of dirt."

Auriol sat silent, battered by conflicting inclinations: desire to contradict, knowledge of its falseness and futility and—worst of all—knowledge of her own inner concurrence with Maggie's diagnosis. The pause, which could hold nothing good, stretched out and out; at the end of it Maggie drew a deep breath, stirred, and returned her eyes to her companion.

"That's that," she said, and something new dawned on Auriol. Maggie, the invincible Maggie: under the composure and dignity with which she had sustained the blow, she was terrified. As the other contemplated this with a sort of unbelief—

"Well, mate, we've had it," Maggie was speaking again. "We'd just better part brass rags, from now on."

"Wha—what do you mean?" Auriol gasped foolishly.

"I'd better not see you, you'd better not see me. If we can't do it in the ordinary way, we won't do it at all. Or keeping in touch by stealth, that's out, so far as I'm concerned." She spoke without rancour, not letting go a vestige of her absolute control. "Ordinary messes I've never tried to avoid, but this sort of thing—malice on the scale that can finish me and my business—it's not worth it. Calculated malice, too," she added. "He hated me on sight, and he's promising himself a jolly old time with this. For no better reason than dear Ivor's sense of humour, let myself be ruined? It's you that's let this crypto-lunatic into your life," she pointed out with ruthless clarity, "not I."

"But—but—" Auriol groped, herself surprised at the cold scared void of loneliness that had opened in her heart; she had not experienced anything comparable on leaving Ivor. "Maggie, after all these years," she appealed clumsily. "It's not my—I mean—"

"Sorry," returned Maggie, aloof and implacable, "but there it is." She threw a couple of five-pound notes on the table and rose; her round face and thick sturdy body looked somehow withered. "Come on, let's get to hell out of here."

Silent, Auriol followed her from the restaurant, the small festive bar and vestibule, and through the revolving door. Outside it was damp and warmish; reflection of the street lights were moons, fuzzy and dim, in the wet pavements.

"Where're you going now?" Auriol asked foolishly, from her pit of abandonment. "Home?"

"Presently," Maggie returned. "But first I reckon to look for a nice quiet gutter. Where," she explained politely and formally, "I can lose my dinner in privacy," and Auriol watched as she trudged down the short darkish street and turned the corner.

9

She opened the unrevealing envelope and read her solicitor's letter. The petition had been allowed; they could proceed with the suit on special grounds. But this permission opened before her eyes such vistas of uncertainty and complication that they could scarcely be more endless if the petition had been refused.

The cobbles of the mews were black and slippery under the listless rain; she had not thought to feel them under her feet, ever again. With automatic caution, caroming slightly off their inequalities every now and again, she advanced with downbent head and sombre look, wrapped in reflection; blind to all but her own complacent stupidity, her immovable, obtuse conviction —that she must hear from Ivor, that he must be as chafed and restless as herself with their unresolved situation, and anxious—at least after a period—to get in touch with her . . . He had not got in touch with her, nor—it dawned on her finally—nor would he. Then followed the interval, exhausting and infuriating, when by letters, by phone calls that were part insistences and part appeals, she had pinned him to this interview; incredibly, he had seemed indifferent whether they met or not. This was so utterly out of character as she knew his character, or thought she knew it, that even with her growing rage a bewilderment filled her. *He can't want it to go on like this,* was her endless formula of attempted understanding, concluded at last by an iteration equally endless: *He's making me come to him.* And her first violent response, *I'll see him in hell first,* yielded gradually to another, still violent but more factual: *All right, I'll go to him. If I've got to, I will.* She must submit to everything: to swallow her pride, her defiances, the searing injustice of being the wronged party yet having to make all the capitulations. She was the one who could wear herself out with effort; he had only to remain quiescent and tranquil and watch her threshing and struggling in the net . . .

Maggie was suddenly in her mind, an unwelcome guest, along with a sense of loss whose dimensions she could not have guessed; her resentment against Maggie veered to Ivor, became hot and rushing . . . simultaneously she warned herself that to arrive there, already churned up and quivering to launch an offensive, would be worse than useless. She must be pleasant, she must maintain an equanimity against whatever provocation. And again with somnambulistic gait and closed blank face she moved along under an unseen duress, because she could not help herself.

She touched the bell, and waited. The house seemed entirely dark, but she knew how effectively the curtains muffled it. If the Patchams were there it would be awkward; she wanted no one within hearing. Since one of them had not answered by now, probably they were at the cinema, where they frequently went in the evenings. Shifting from one foot to the other, she canvassed two possibilities. First, that no one was home at all; that Ivor had made the appointment and simply gone out, leaving her to come to an empty house. It would be like him. Second, that he was there and was deliberately making her wait; it would be like him also. She settled down grimly to stand there as long as was necessary to make sure one way or the other. Ring a second time she would not; if anyone were in, the bell had been heard.

And the silence and darkness held unbroken, the damp was unpleasant in her nostrils, there was a slight chill movement in the night air . . .

The door came open with no least preliminary sound of footsteps or fastenings being undone; it was disconcerting. Wordlessly she passed over the threshold in response to his wordless stepping aside, thinking that her second guess had been right; he had let her cool her heels while he took his time, how contemptible . . . there, she was working herself up to anger again, the very thing she must not, must not do . . .

"Give me your coat," he said, as she preceded him into the living-room.

"No thanks," she said too curtly, then tried to soften it with, "It's not heavy, and I think I've a bit of a chill."

"You won't be chilly in here," he returned, ignoring her oblique reference to her sojourn on his door-mat. "Let me have it."

She hesitated, then let him help her out of the coat if only to cut short this idiotic parley; again how like him, knowing she could have come here only for urgent reasons, to have mired them already in these trivialities.

"Thank you," she was compelled to follow the lead of polite commonplace that he had established. At once, also, she felt how it undermined her impetus and purpose, and realized with what calculation he did it.

"Sit down," he was saying. "Will you have coffee? a drink?"

"No, no." A driving restlessness was suddenly all through her, a desire to tear free from his elegant, leisured cobweb. "Let's talk, let's—"

"Well, don't fume," he interrupted mildly. "Fuming never yet advanced anything, I promise you."

"I'm not fuming," she muttered untruthfully, and recognized the veiled warning. He would not be pushed, everything must be done at his pace, not hers; any pressure upon him would ricochet on herself in the shape of defeat. She must walk a chalk line, she must bridle herself sufficiently to match her step with his, and even more insistently the inward tocsin dinned, *Don't lose your temper, don't, don't.*

"Sit down," he invited pleasantly.

"I'd rather stand." Restive, she shook her head. "I can talk better standing."

"I can't listen better, though." He smiled. "It distracts me. Please sit down."

She hesitated again, then took the nearest chair.

"There?" he queried. "Must you be uncomfortable?"

"Ivor," she returned in a measured voice. "Please, for God's sake please. What difference does it make whether the chair's—" she bit it off abruptly, unclenching her teeth and wondering what harm her small spurt of uncontrol had done her. Nor did he trouble to enlighten her, merely regarding her with unimpaired affability and leaving it all to her—silence, talk, choice of subject; the whole weight of the interview.

"I haven't heard from you all this time, and I thought—" she began infelicitously, and stopped again. "I mean, after all this time—I thought I'd have heard from you by now."

"Did you?" he queried amiably, and raised his eyebrows. "And why should you have expected to hear from me?"

With all her experience of him and his tactics, she was still dumbstruck; still bludgeoned to earth by incredulity, by the mammoth dimension of his wrongmindedness.

"Well," she articulated after a momen , "with matters as they are, surely you . . . surely . . . I mean, things can't simply go on like this, c they? They've got to be settled one way or another aven't they—for your sake as well as mine?" she pr ded, as his affable surface seemed undisturbed by ny disposition to answer. *Damn him,* she panted silently, *letting me do it all, damn him.* "Haven't they, Ivor?"

"My dear," he returned, caressingly almost. "The present state of affairs between us is not of my making. And as I had no hand in bringing it about—"

A gasp shook her inwardly; her chief concern was whether it had been overt enough for him to notice.

"—in consequence I feel no obligation to resolve it. So why should you expect to hear from me? why should *I* be the one to make the gesture?"

"But—but—" she floundered witlessly; her mind was blank of everything, except that his reasonable voice and look were somehow a mortal affront.

"No." He seemed a little bored. "I decline to involve myself, by so much as lifting a finger. The situation being all yours, I leave it in your hands." He gestured a total deference to her. "Entirely. It's yours, it's up to you."

The pause that followed was itself an admission of checkmate, if not of unqualified defeat. But defeat at this point was impossible; somehow she must rally, find arguments so persuasive, so insinuating, that they would melt instead of reinforce his resistance, so deep-rooted *so wrong* . . . She ignored a fainting doubt as to whether such arguments existed, and resumed in a supplicating voice, "Ivor."

He looked at her, receptive and polite, not betraying his enjoyment of her begging voice, and he had no need to; she could feel it without seeing it.

"We're fairly young, both of us," she went on with painful reasonableness. "We may live thirty or forty years yet. Leaving me out of it, you can't simply want to be stuck in the middle of a . . . an unresolved situation that keeps you all alone, keeps you from being interested in anyone else, if you wanted to be. Think of it!" she implored, too vehemently. "For years, Ivor, for all those years!"

If mockery underlay his courteous and attentive air, she must not think of it at this stage.

"You'd like a family, you'd like children—"

Consternation cut her off like a garrotte; sitting silent, in their ears echoed her wounding mirth of not too long ago, her unforgivable laughter.

"—you're young, you're attractive." Shutting away

106

her sense of disaster, she stumbled on in clumsy desperate propitiation. "You could marry someone else, and be happy. Happier at any rate than you were with me, God knows."

The corners of his mouth, all but imperceptibly, had moved upward; did she hear the silent answer, *And by that token so might you be happy, if I let you go free. But I don't choose that you should be free and happy . . . ?*

"That—that special suit we were talking of, that time," she laboured on perforce. "I can bring it, I've petitioned and I've been allowed. 'It's my—it's our chance for a quick divorce, a decent one. No sordid grounds, no one gets hurt—"

She canvassed his face, unrevealing as his utter, amiable silence.

"—so I—I was hoping—"

"What were you hoping?" he encouraged gently, as she stopped again.

"—for—for your assurance that you won't defend. Ivor, please, please, I beg you." She had forgotten to resent her naked beggary; willingly she assumed it. "I simply haven't the money to go up against a defended action. No money and no time, either—I've got to make my living. Ivor, if you'd promise me not to defend, I'd be so—so very, very"—still she was abject and still she did not care—"grateful."

"But naturally I'll defend." His cool, decided tone was quite without animus. "Did you expect I'd simply lie down under such an aspersion?"

"But there *is* no aspersion." Over an icy qualm of dismay, she fought on. "We spoke about it, don't you remember, there's no reflection on either of us, it's merely—it's incompatibility, that's all it amounts to, really—"

"Does it? I haven't your facility of legal definition. Not having availed myself of expert advice"—he smiled—"like you."

"Certainly I've taken advice." Now her fear was belligerence; fear that his tactics would goad her into breaking out at him savagely. And the day was triply lost if she did that, she must not, must not . . . "What else did you expect?"

"Ah, let's not waste time on *my* poor expectations," he murmured, and the burlesque humility roused her to demand, "D'you think I'll take that for an answer?"

"Perhaps not," he returned, always equable. "Very well, I'll do my best to make my position clear." He paused for an instant; when he resumed, his tone was at least purged of its covert derision. "During the period that you absent yourself from this house, which is your home, and whatever you choose to do during that period, I shan't divorce you. Whatever your behaviour, whatever cause you supply, I shan't divorce you. I stand ready, always, to take back my—ah—possibly erring wife"—the mockery gleamed through for an instant— "and forgive her for all and any indiscretions. For desertion. For adultery, if any. For submitting to undesirable or improper influence."

The oblique allusion to Maggie touched her like a cold finger; afraid to goad him into developing it by comment of any kind, she waited.

"And if you go ahead with this incompatibility thing or whatever you call it," he was saying, "I'll defend to the last ditch, and I don't care at all how much money I spend. People," he enunciated with a clarity quite passionless, yet biting, "don't do these things to me—and other things—and get away with it."

"What other things?" she asked in utter bewilderment. "What have I done to you, Ivor? What other things?"

"Oh, nothing." He was airy. "Nothing."

"Nothing—how dare—you think you can make these cowardly accusations, and not explain them?"

"But assuredly." His eyes were wide, his tone ingenuous. "If I choose."

"What have I done to you?" she fought him, almost inaudible from breathlessness. "Tell me. Tell me—!"

"Hush," he murmured, with forbearance and distaste combined. "Your persistence, my dear—tiresome."

She took a moment to fight her way from the splintered wreckage that he could always make of sense and reason, then said, "All right." She got to her feet with no sign of her inward violence; her voice fell lower. "All right. If that's your last word, here's mine. You've made your position clear, I'll make mine clear too."

Chief in her consciousness, incongruously, was the muffled quality of the scene; its quiet, in contrast to the first divorce talk between them, when her clamour and invective had filled the room.

"There's another thing I can do," she pursued in the same dry, dwindled voice. "I hadn't wanted even to mention it, my only thought was to spare you. I was hoping you'd be civilized about it—I should have known better." A half-smile dawned darkly in her face, a baleful threat. "I'll sue you on what they call a nullity. Not consummating a marriage. Impotence."

He sat perfectly still, looking at her, nor was this stillness like the stillness of his habitual repose. The silence, too, was different; a black silence, like Arctic night.

"I'll give you . . . two months . . . to make up your mind." The pause in which she seemed to debate the period of grace was spurious; she herself needed those two months to bring up her financial reserves. Moreover, she needed them so badly that she experienced an apprehensive shrinking that his antennae would pick up some sense of this urgency. He could see thought itself sometimes, or so it appeared . . .

"Two months," she repeated. "I'll give you every chance. All I want from you is to let the cruelty thing go through undefended. If you won't"—she had to stop for breath—"I'll do the other. If you force me, I'll do it."

His eyes looking at her were like the silence, full of night. Now she was chiefly conscious of his eyes.

"I see," he observed at last, softly. "Well, there seems little or nothing that I can say."

"It's not my fault." The let-down was upon her, the

collapse of the hatred that had borne her up to this point. She stood looking dully at the ground; there was a pause. Into it—

"Divorce, I believe, is at best an expensive business," he let fall meditatively. "Who's to produce the money for all this? Not you, you've nothing aside from what you're paid. Who makes up the lack? Mummy?"

Her heart stood still; a sharp indrawn breath escaped her.

"Got it," he congratulated himself affably. "In one, didn't I?"

"No," she contravened, scarcely able to get the word out. That he would seize on her self-betraying gasp she had known, but not that it would lend itself to such misinterpretation. "No! she's nothing at all to do with—with—"

"Mummy to the rescue," he murmured dulcetly. "Mummy will help."

At the thought of her mother, fragile and defenceless, incurring this unplumbed hostility, a light-headedness of fear took her—yet the worst of it was over in a moment. Whatever his twisted grievances against Mrs. Chapman, there was no way he could touch a semi-recluse who never left her flat, except in her daughter's company. And her daughter would make it a point to be in still closer attendance, she thought grimly but fleetingly, as the present need—the overwhelming present need—bore down on her in all its urgency. At all costs she must deprecate having had the upper hand for a moment, she must defer to him, propitiate, set him up again in his ascendancy . . .

"Ivor," she supplicated. "Please, please believe that my mother has absolutely nothing to do with all this. Actually she doesn't even know about it, I haven't said anything to her—" she broke off short with the shapeless fear that she should not have told him this, that he would turn it to account God knew how; every word spoken to this man was a risk, a step into an uncharted dark . . . No use now; she had thought of it too late, and hurried past her apprehension as if it were a graveyard at night.

"Everything I'm doing in this is my own responsibility," she averred with emphasis. "It's mine, and no one else's. And I'm sorry, I'm so sorry—about the—the nullity. I never wanted it to come up, never, but you—you forced—I mean—"

He had risen, terminating the interview. The disconcerting effect was maximum, as usual; all in the same instant and without a word cutting her short, evicting her from the room, and impelling her down the hall.

"Ivor." Like a fool she made a last attempt, standing on the doorstep. "I'm sorry, sorry—"

The door shut in her face without a sound.

10

Naked duress, the thought of outright compulsion used against any living creature, was hateful to her; yet she had used it against Ivor. And the fact that he had virtually compelled her, that his tactics would compel extremity of measure from anyone, failed to sustain or reassure her. Improbable that substantial retaliation was within his power, yet she continued uneasy. And beyond the uneasiness—she realized belatedly—was something even more oppressive, the worse for being indefinable; a gnawing on the edges of her conscience like a mouse on the edges of sleep, but what was it? She defined the feeling after some thought, then pushed away the definition with indignation and belligerence. Guilt? Toward *him*, of all people? Her conscience, aggressively clear, stiffened her with all the moral rectitude of the innocent and injured party. Yet on the edges of her mind continued that faint gnawing, that recall to a fretting wakefulness.

The door of her office opened, and Tom walked in with a sheaf of galleys in his hand. In that moment, oddly, it struck her that his tallness and ruggedness were attractive. She was not usually drawn to tall or powerful-looking men, liking such qualities in degree, but now she found them in refreshing contrast to the feline elegance which for months had been her sole masculine diet; perhaps not masculine, only male, and was it even male . . . ?

"How many plates," he saluted her, "are they giving the Pennington job?"

"Eight," she said, "as usual."

"Where the hell do I get eight good plates for that period?" he demanded gloomily, shaking his head in exasperation; a heavy spike of nondescript blond hair fell toward one eye. "Have to fake it, I expect—prints of naval engagements, Charles One and the Dook—do it that way."

"I know," she said, understanding his discontent accurately, then all at once realized the source of the attractiveness in him that she had found so unusual.

"Tom," she voiced a question uncommon in their relationship, which was cordial but impersonal. "Haven't you lost weight?"

Just on his way to the door he stopped dead and presented her, for the fraction of a second, with his motionless back.

"I might have done," he said casually, turning again. "A bit."

"Well, don't put it on again," she adjured. "You look almost handsome this way."

He smiled absently, scanning her piled desk, then in his turn asked, "You've the hell of a load here—full-time. Doesn't the lord and master object?"

"No," she lied automatically and without thinking, protecting her privacy. None of her associates knew of her position, not even her employer, nor did she find it necessary that they should. Personal confidences were not her habit, except with Maggie, and even with Maggie they had been limited.

"No? dashed reasonable of him," said Tom. She could see him trying to square this reasonableness with his recollection of Ivor, and failing. "Because we've pretty long hours here. He doesn't object at all?"

He doesn't object at all, she intended to say, but only

her lips moved; in a sudden engulfing desolation, she sat staring at her desk.

"Roly! are you all right?"

Tom's voice broke the capsule of blankness that held her, as if she had gone under ether for a moment; trying to emerge from it, she could only come halfway.

"What is it?" He was alarmed. "Roly, wake up!"

"I'm awake," she managed with an unsteady laugh. "Just—giddy for a moment."

"Giddy my foot. What is it? What's wrong?"

"Nothing, nothing." With something near panic she was aware of her overwhelming need to talk to someone, then snatched at her habit of reticence just in time and said stubbornly, "I'm perfectly all right."

"Come on, old girl," he ignored her disclaimer. "What is it? What's the matter?"

His tone was the final blow at her defences, fatally eroded by Maggie's withdrawal. Persuasion she could dismiss, urgency she could ignore, but not the comforting quality in his voice; it was the comfort that undid her.

"I've left Ivor," she said, completely against her intention.

He waited for something more, apparently; when it failed to come he ventured, "A quarrel, do you mean? a spat?"

"Spat!" Her echo was ironic. "I've left him once and for all. Finally."

Noncommittal, he was taking this in; when he spoke at last his voice might have made her angry if she'd been in a condition to notice it, it was so full of concern —and worse; full of compassion. "But you're still in love with him?"

"No." She laughed briefly, checking her inclination to say, *As if I'd ever been in love with him.* "Good God, no."

"All that's wrong with you is . . . the general wreckage, you mean? Aftermath?"

"That's all."

"I see." His soothing voice had turned brisk; he seemed to take hold of the situation from another angle. "You need a little diversion," he prescribed decisively. "Have dinner with me tonight, will you? Can you?"

"Oh, Tom, that would be lovely." The dullness and remoteness that were about to close on her again opened wide like curtains. Amazing, how heart-warming was this small prospect of cheer and companionship; it could make no real impression on the bleakness, yet it buoyed her up disproportionately—until she remembered, and asked, "What about Christine?"

"She's away."

"But if she happened to hear of your taking me out" —awkwardly she demurred, the nymph in silver-green satin all at once vivid in her mind; the spoiled, petted, avid nymph—"won't she mind?"

"She won't mind." The flatness of the declaration might have reached her if she herself had not been reaching too greedily for the slight surcease from her trouble.

"Well, then, it would be lovely," she repeated. "Thank you."

"There's a little place in Old Brompton Road called Lucerne, run by Swiss. Not bad. In fact, it's damned good. I'll book, h'm? And meet you there at eight?"

"Your coffee's better than that restaurant swill," said Tom.

"Not much recommendation," she pointed out, "at that."

"Badly phrased, badly phrased. But at that place the food's always good and the coffee's always dishwater. Odd, isn't it?"

"Yes, like another place I know, the meat and chicken are excellent and the vegetables are vile. Just a peculiarity of restaurants, I expect."

"So here's where you've retreated." While they made talk about restaurants he had been appraising her domain, with its furnished-rental look like the mark of

115

Cain. "It's a come-down, I'll bet. No wonder you needed a little cheer."

"The come-down I don't mind, and of course it's not gay," she returned. "But it's what I can afford. And not cheap, let me tell you."

"Well, anyway, let's join forces again when you feel like it," he offered companionably. "Dinner or theatre or a film."

"Tom," she said fervently, wanting to cry out of mere gratitude, "I can't tell you what a comfort, what a *comfort*—"

"Comfort's very important," he agreed gravely. "When you need it."

She was silent, caught for an instant in a complicated mesh of reminiscence. Her first loneliness at Maggie's defection had yielded, long since, to something more erosive: a desolate wonderment that a woman so tough as Maggie, a despiser of coercion, should nevertheless let herself be coerced and pushed around by Ivor. What a demonstration of his baneful power to wither and distort, even at a remove . . .

"Well, when you're at a low ebb"—Tom had risen—"just knock me up and we'll do something about it."

"Darling Tom," she muttered, her voice not very steady. Amazing how hungrily her heart, a castaway on a raft, reached out for this temporary ally and fleeting solace; what a difference it made to everything. "Well, if Christine doesn't object to charity, and until she comes back—"

"Yes."

"It's been such a lovely evening." She put her arms around his neck and kissed him. "Thank you, thank you."

"Don't come down," he protested at the door of her flat.

"The halls're dark as pitch and you don't know where the lights are." She went past him. "I don't mind escorting you."

She stood for a moment inside the street door as he descended from the portico.

"Good night!" he called at the bottom of the steps.

"Good night!" she returned eagerly. "Dear, dear Tom, good night!"

11

The envelope, fortunately, had attracted her attention from the first moment.

In the well-kept house that contained her mother's flat, mail for the tenants was deployed in orderly fashion on a hall table. It was Auriol's invariable custom, on arriving, to scan the display and take anything that had come for Mrs. Chapman, who—as is customary in the dwindling world of the old, and as time went on—received fewer and fewer letters. Routine bills were the bulk of her communication, with an occasional missive from ancient cousins; anything more was in the nature of an event. But the envelope which had struck her, whether an event or not, had about it something inexplicable, at least in connection with the person to whom it was addressed. It was poor quality, wrinkled and grubby-looking, and inscribed in a laborious hand that she classified, on first sight, as illiterate; in any correspondence sent to her mother, she had never seen anything like it.

For a long moment she stood there holding it, her aspect puzzled and indecisive. Once her nostrils twitched slightly, unconsciously, as if picking up some taint; afterward she was to wonder if the nose were indeed sensitive to immaterial corruption. At the moment she only hesitated, then obeyed some indefinable instinct and—right or wrong—tore open the envelope. It contained only a single sheet of paper, poor quality and soiled-looking like the envelope, and folded once.

Your daugter is a whore, it began. *Fine daugter you got, wants plenty men. And you help her get them you old bitch dont you, you dirty old sow—*

It fell into such obscenity that her head began to swim and turn light as she read, feeling it all to be unreal, something that would turn out to have been nightmare . . . The bit of soft grimy paper in her hand said otherwise, and already her first shock and bewilderment were turning to something else. Not the realization that by such an act Ivor had played into her hands, had himself furthered and expedited the divorce she was seeking; the divorce was wiped as clean from her mind as if it never had been, and in its place was something purely, intensely personal: an icy murderous hatred. In that instant all her intention of saving her husband's face, of protecting his pride, shrivelled like grass before a flame-thrower. She wanted to expose him, brand him. Any attack on herself she could forgive, but for this there was no forgiveness; nor could there be any doubt that this horror emanated from him, in spite of the unrecognizable hand and the calculated misspellings. She drew a loud harsh breath in the empty hall, groping meanwhile for any means, any expedients, since now and at once she must grapple with the emergency . . . with her head still spinning, after a moment she pressed the caretaker's bell, then all at once found her legs would no longer support her, and sat down suddenly on one of the hall chairs, springless and hard.

The light went on behind the ribbed-glass screen that closed off the basement stairway, and ascending steps heralded the appearance of Mrs. Williams, small and neat, with her cosy stoutness and ready, obliging air. She was the widow of a retired Admiralty Messenger, and Auriol had always considered her salt of the earth. But how explain to anyone, however obliging, a thing like this?

"Mrs. Williams," she appealed perforce, after greetings. "Please do something for me. Will you collect *all* letters for my mother, anything at all that comes in the post? Just keep it downstairs, and I'll pick it up every evening and take it to her—I'll come specially."

"Why, yes, I'll do that, madam," said Mrs. Williams willingly, yet this very concurrence might enclose some seed of casualness or forgetfulness, and Auriol was driven to be specific; the woman must understand, partly at least, the urgency of the matter.

"I wouldn't ask you," she pursued, "but it seems as though someone's trying to frighten her. I opened this just on—on a hunch—and if she'd seen it, I don't know what would have happened. I—I honestly don't know, Mrs. Williams."

"Isn't that dreadful," said Mrs. Williams placidly. "I'll certainly do that, madam. Sometimes I don't come up straightaway when I hear the post, but now I'll watch out specially."

"Oh, thank you." Auriol was fervent. "I wouldn't give you the trouble, but this is terribly serious."

"Very glad to help." Mrs. Williams with all her sympathy still looked and sounded cheerful and tranquil, a lucky woman incapable of emotion, from whatever stress.

"I'm afraid we'll have to keep it up," said Auriol grimly, "till I've found out who's responsible."

"That's all right," acquiesced Mrs. Williams. "Oh! that's very good of you, madam."

"I'll count on you," Auriol petitioned, and the other promised, "Don't worry, I'll keep a sharp lookout. Dear me, the wickedness there is in the world, isn't there then?"

Mild and tidy, of instinctive rectitude and integrity, she retreated again to her basement. She had been handsomely recompensed, but Auriol knew she would have done the same service without a penny, kind civil Mrs. Williams, a type disappearing.

The words *anonymous letters* over the phone, like a penny dropping, produced with remarkable promptitude her first contact with the law outside of greetings to the constable on the beat, in the shape of Detective-Sergeant Cornworthy. He was fortyish, greyish, and reminded her of a senior clerk or some such functionary, with the same sober and overworked look. Unexpectedly, the first thing that steadied her was his unmoved reading of the letter without comment, either of surprise or disgust, and she reminded herself that the event, so shattering to her, was commonplace to him; nastiness and abomination were his daily fare. And logically or not, his manner helped to restore her sense of proportion.

"Yes, very good," he said, raising his head after a first perusal. "And this is the first one there's been? I see. Now let me ask you, madam, have you any definite suspicions of where this comes from?"

"My husband—from whom I've separated," she returned promptly, and under the spur of his inquiring gaze sketched the situation. "I don't see how it can be anyone else," she concluded. "He didn't want me to leave, and I don't doubt that he'll get back at me in any way he can, even"—her voice turned raw—even like this. About myself I don't care, but my mother—who's ill—"

"Quite, madam," he returned, and again his beneficent calm soothed her. "Now, would you have in your possession any of this gentleman's writing? letters and so on?"

As her startled hesitation showed how completely she had overlooked this point, he went on, "We must have something for purposes of comparison, and the more the better."

Dismayed, about to deny such ownership—for they had never corresponded, there had been no need—she was rescued by a sudden, miraculous thought.

"I have the stubs from one of his cheque-books," she

offered. "How it came to be among my things I don't know, and I don't *expect* I've thrown it away."

Sergeant Cornworthy, when she had put this meagre offering in his hands, looked it over with a dissatisfied and dubious eye. "It's not very much," he deplored. "Notations on a cheque-stub, they're mostly figures, aren't they? Still, it's better than nothing. And your husband's name and address, madam? and occupation?" His manner, increasingly thoughtful as he noted down the expensive neighbourhood and gentlemanly profession, silently served notice on her that such an objective must be explored with that extreme of tact reserved for the rich and reputable. "Well, I'll see what we can do with this, and let you know. And any further communications of this nature, you'll let us have them?"

"I certainly shall," she returned, then realized how heavily she was banking on the interceptive power of Mrs. Williams; suppose by some mishap she failed once, only once, but once would be enough. A chill went through her as she added virulently, "With pleasure."

Just at the door, the Sergeant turned to impart a last consideration.

"I must warn you," he apologized, "that our handwriting expert's always over his head in work, so all this may take some little time. And I'm afraid he'll consider that he's got very little to work on. Well, never mind. Thank you, madam, good day to you."

That a blind spot probably dwells in every living being, had long been one of her convictions. A blind spot or some form of stupidity, and she was well aware of her own: that it often took her a long time to wake up to obvious things. This was the case in the present instance, that her tension and dread on her mother's account were infiltrated, only after days, by dread on her own account, and this dread was largely mixed with puzzlement. Ivor had demonstrated against Mrs. Chapman because he believed she was financing his wife's divorce, but even so Mrs. Chapman was subordinate in the affair; herself, Auriol, was the principal character, and should be the principal target. Why had he made no move of retaliation against her—yet? That *yet* she recognized as the key word; it was certain that he would coil and strike—in his own good time. What form this thrust from the darkness would take, she could not even guess.

Thinking of it she had acquired, unconsciously, a cringing movement of the neck and shoulders. Against this her feeble remedy was not to think about it, so far as she could keep from thinking about it. If only she could anticipate the character of the blow, the direction from which it would come . . . as impossible to predict, though, as the workings of that unpredictable sterile brilliance, that distillery of sharpest unease. She could only cower beneath the hovering shadow; cower and wait.

The door of her small office was pushed open; not raising her head from the proofs she was marking, with pleasure she recognized the dimensions of the shoes and legs.

"Be with you in a moment, Tom," she said amiably but absently. "Sit down."

When her eyes, released, had climbed to the level of his, the pleasure drained from her like water from a sieve; a sort of shock took her, and beyond the shock a dull recognition, even salutation: *Here it is, here it comes, whatever it is*. Already, before the blow fell, she knew without knowing, prepared by the forbidding quality of his face.

"I've had a slight encounter," he began grimly. "When I left last night, your husband was waiting for me just outside the door. Came up and spoke to me—I'd barely seen let alone recognized him, it was too dark."

In the same leaden prescience, she waited.

"He told me to let you alone or he'd make trouble for

123

me," Tom continued. "He knew I'd been up to your flat the other night—had the hours down pat and reeled them off to me, like a copper with his little notebook."

He must have been waiting there when we arrived, her numb heart supplied in antiphon. *He watches me then. I'd no idea . . .*

"He's watching you all the time, apparently," Tom went on, in comfortless echo of her own thought. "At any rate he said he'd begin by registering his protest with my employers. He said he was perfectly aware that my private life is none of their affair, but all the same they wouldn't fancy it much, the prospect of his naming me in a legal action. And he's quite right—they wouldn't."

Nothing that made sense occurred to her, yet she tried to speak, and produced from her painful throat only a sort of croak. It made no difference though; he had not paused for an answer but to sort out the rest of his narrative; he was quite unaware of her effort.

"He wasn't ugly about it, you understand," he resumed. "No raised voice, no gestures, all of it quiet, conversational, as nice and polite as you please. Lovely faultless manners—made it worse somehow."

Again, acquiescent, she registered this echo of her own response to that inhuman, flawless courtesy.

"Well, you see where this puts us." He was pursuing the thought, after a pause. "If he says we're having an affair, we've no defence."

A vestige of argument passed through her mind too fleetingly to be pinned, and was gone.

"Except denial," he went on. "Which is good enough to make a cat laugh, but not much good otherwise. So—"

He paused again, and she was intimately aware of the nature of the pause. He was trying to soften the dismissal by summoning a kinder inflection into his voice, which had been of a controlled hostility; he blamed her, while aware that his blame was unjust. He himself had invited this consequence of his idea of dinner and an evening together, and would now like to make the severance as little wounding as possible.

"—so you see"—he summed it up—"our idea of getting together now and again—we'd better scrub it out. We can't do anything however harmless, dinner, the cinema, anything, without having this character drop on us. He's out to make trouble, work at having me slung out of my job, God knows what. A thing like that, you can't take it on. There're limits—it's not worth it."

"No," she agreed. "It's not worth it."

"Well, you yourself see, don't you?" A defensive note had entered his voice. "If I thought he were crazy I could brush him off, but he's anything but crazy. Or if he is"—he qualified, on sudden afterthought—"I don't like the variety—cold and clear, clear as crystal. That kind frightens me. Actually, you know, the man's dangerous."

Unable to contradict the proposition, she sat wordless.

"Sorry, Auriol."

In all the years they had known each other, he had never called her Auriol; with that perverse spark of irony that presumably lingers in the human mind till the very moment of extinction, she saw this usage as honouring the full-dress farewell, like the special language used for obsequies.

"Sorry," he was repeating, "but what else—? Nothing to do but be sensible. Damned sorry," he iterated, and moved toward the door.

Out of a reminiscent desolation that had taken her on an earlier occasion when she had been dropped, out of a half-hallucination where Maggie spoke and Tom said the same words after her like a Greek chorus, unexpectedly there intruded itself a clear thought: the argument that had fleetingly grazed her before, then vanished.

"Tom," she said suddenly.

Not turning, he stopped with his hand on the knob.

"Tom, I only just thought of it," she pursued almost eagerly. "Ivor'll get nowhere, saying things about you and me. Everyone knows you're in love with another woman—everyone knows you're engaged to her."

Even the lines of his back seemed to change, heralding the other change as he faced her.

"I *am* in love with another woman," he agreed. The hostility he would not show before was now overt not in his voice only, but in his face. He hated her for extorting the admission from him, and in a flash of belated recognition she saw it all: the reason for the new angularity of his well-padded frame, the bleakness and darkening of his cheerful easy-going look: also her own blindness, her stupidity.

"But an engagement that's done with, that's nothing we can hide behind. Christine and I broke up three weeks ago."

A new thought struck him visibly and hard.

"Why, Hailes can even say she broke it off because I took up with you." It had begun as soliloquy and ended as accusation. "It fits in, everything works for him. It all fits in so well." He swung about and seized the knob once more. "So damned well."

The door closed behind him.

12

The ringing blasted her out of sleep, the complete established sleep of the small hours; waking, confusion, panic, were almost simultaneous. She groped for the bedside lamp with disorganized hands against the piercing double note that went on and on, for this could be nothing but bad news. This must be her mother's doctor or Mrs. Williams the caretaker, routed out of bed by emergency . . .

"Hello!" she managed, over her pounding heart, then heard the signal that meant a public phone, with the caller ready to make the connection with his three-pence. Instantly her ready imagination offered a picture still more ominous; of illness not only sudden but so grave that her mother's bedside phone could not be used; this then was the house phone, which was of the coin variety. Already in her mind she had scrambled from bed and into clothes, already she was in the night streets looking for a taxi . . .

"Hello?" she repeated, more and more frightened. Now the pips had ceased, the caller would speak. She listened, waiting and nonplussed at the silence, then hazarded, "Mummy? Mrs. Williams?" Straining her ears against the emptiness, with puzzlement slowly displacing shock, she gasped, Who is it?"

Silence again; then, from the humming void, the

merest ghost of a laugh or a chuckle, yet too insubstantial for either. Grotesquely the thought brushed her that if a smile could be heard, this was how it would sound. In the same moment, and with no impact of a replaced receiver, the dialling tone came on again.

She rang off, then with slow trammelled movements looked at her watch. Quarter past three. She switched off the lamp and lay back, wide awake in the darkness. This was most likely some sort of mechanical accident, yet perhaps not; it was remarkable how many women of her acquaintance, most living alone, had received obscene phone calls at all sorts of hours. Not very pleasant, the thought that some perverted walker of the night had signalled his further intentions with this first metallic intrusion. However, nothing to do: nothing but wait and see.

Almost too tired to nibble at the prospect with worry or even conjecture, she dismissed it and lay regretting her beautiful sleep, the harbour where all her anxieties and uncertainties, her growing sense of loneliness, were drowned in the soothing dark. Dull and inert, yet awoken past recall she lay wide-eyed, and instantly a new vision came to haunt her—a vision as recent as yesterday, when she had stepped into the entrance hall of Mrs. Chapman's flat, and seen, with lurching heart, her mother standing at the table where the post was left, looking the envelopes over. Here was dismaying proof that Mrs. Chapman emerged from her rooms oftener than might be suspected, and that the double precaution of her daughter's daily visits and Mrs. Williams' vigilance might be reduced, by merely unlucky chance, to nothing. And the vista opened by this proof could only be of potential undisclosed but bad, all bad . . .

More than ever awake she twisted sharply in the dark, assessing her mother's appearance as she remembered it. Mrs. Chapman had seemed her accustomed self, showing no sign of disturbance overt or otherwise. Obviously the daily interception and inspection of her letters had been successful, up till now; yet her presence in the hall demonstrated how easily, by a matter of seconds, she might find herself face to face with obscene malignity.

And yet, in spite of it, the driven-off sleep was there; weariness submerged her. Sighing deeply then yawning she turned on her side, shifting till she lay comfortably, and was grateful that in a few moments she was caught and held again by the precious obliterating drowsiness.

Just on the verge of sleep, the phone bell woke her again.

Sergeant Cornworthy's "some little time" proved a euphemism; still, he had warned her. During the long period when she waited to hear from him, the nocturnal summons in her sleeping ear, the shrill invitation to nothing and no one, began unpredictably and ceased unpredictably, sometimes for so long she dared to hope it was over—except, of course, that it was not over. In connection with it, but not till many repetitions, another thing dawned on her: that these calls were most apt to come on a rainy night. This evoked the dark image of an aberration somehow linked to rain and stirred to action by rain, as it was once thought that madness was stirred by the moon. And though reason might decry this fancy, instinct cowered at the dark overhanging thought: the night dripping and black and the shrilling bell; the coalition that was changing her from a young woman of charming appearance to a creature marked by anxiety and harassment and haggard with broken sleep.

The Sergeant's advent, in the final analysis, was cold comfort; the moment she saw him she knew he had nothing for her.

"Well now, madam, I'll tell you," he began in his civil, unvarying manner, having seated himself at her invitation. "I've discussed the matter with our handwriting man. Rather thoroughly, I may say, so's not to overlook anything—myself being *very* anxious to do something about this." The slight stress, coming from his professional impassivity, was enormously significant. "Now about disguised handwriting, there's a theory that it can't stand up to expert tests. That's not true, madam. According to our man, there's hands that can be readily traced to the writer by comparative measurements and so forth, and there's hands that can't be traced at all, not by any existing means. For example, the writing in this letter to your mother can't be connected with your husband, *except* as every characteristic of the letter is directly opposed to every characteristic of his natural hand—a sort of resemblance by opposites, you might say? But that won't wash, madam. It's exactly as though I argued that because everything about yourself, for instance is exactly opposite to everything about a thief, it therefore follows that you *are* a thief. That sort of logic —it won't stand up."

She was silent.

"And if our man says that, about this writing," he added in corollary, "you may rely on his opinion. Our man is consulted on a greater number of questionable documents than anyone else in the world, I reckon."

Part of her noted, with disconsolate amusement, his pride in "our man," then woke with a sort of start to the new inquisition he had set in motion.

"Previous to this, or at any time since," he was asking, "have you been molested in any other way? any way whatever?"

"I'm having some—some other unpleasantness," she admitted, and told the tale of the erratic stridency by night.

"You reported it, quite proper," was his comment.

"Yes, they were so nice about it, they tried in every way to help me, they gave me an ex-directory number straightaway. But that only stopped it for a week," she sighed. "Then the calls began coming again. I was stupid, I expect, to think that anything like that would stop him."

"You attribute these calls also," the Sergeant hazarded delicately, "to your husband—?"

"Who else?" she returned dully, and sat silent; they remained like this for some moments.

"Just so," acquiesced the Sergeant, after the pause. "Well, you may depend on it that they've been monitoring the gentleman's telephone, and that they've turned up nothing whatever. Still, from what I can gather about him—a successful businessman, highly educated —that line of inquiry would be hopeless from the word go."

A deeper trough of silence opened between them; she roused herself from it finally.

"What can I do?" she asked. "What can I do?"

"Well, madam, I'm thinking hard about this, if you'll believe me." His emphasis was solemn. "And it's dicey, very dicey, because there's so little to lay hold of. Suppose you put a private inquiry agent onto the gentleman, to have him followed at nights. And even supposing him to be seen leaving his house and entering a phone-box in the small hours, and things so rigged that you noted the time of the call, such time corresponding with the time he'd made it—well, it's very suggestive indeed, but no absolute proof. There's no law to prevent anyone's using a public phone at any hour of the day or night, and then of course a private agent'd have no authority to charge him or caution him, anything like that. Still, if it was made plain to him that he'd been observed —it might frighten him off that particular caper, at least for a bit."

He glanced at her, seeing from her empty gaze and bowed shoulders how little he had helped.

"Just so, madam," he deprecated to her wordless comment, "it's not much good, I said it wasn't. Especially as you've told me the calls come at irregular intervals, with longish waits in between? Just so," he affirmed, at her nod. "Any tail you put on him might have to keep it up for days or weeks before you could find

131

out anything. And a private agent runs to money—very considerable money, always."

"That's out in any case," she returned. "I couldn't possibly afford it."

"Just so, madam. Well." He rose. "I'm sorry we couldn't do better, very sorry indeed. We'll keep the situation in view, and if in future you could lay your hands on anything in the way of proof—"

He stopped with a shamefaced air, again hearing, obviously, her silent reply, *If you couldn't, how can I?*

"Just so," he re-affirmed; it was a characteristic expression with him, evidently. But at the door, and about to pass through, he gave surprising testimony—he with his imperturbable manner, his professional stolidity—of how hard he was taking this failure.

"I'm no church-goer," he observed, his face so set that for a moment it looked not flesh but granite, "yet I was brought up very strictly in the Church of England, if you'll believe me. And with all the times I've read the Commination in the Prayerbook, it seems to me I only just now understand the part where it goes"—an angry red came up on his cheekbones—" 'Cursed is he that smiteth his neighbour secretly.' Good day to you, madam."

13

"Mummy," she ventured in a guarded voice, not knowing whether or not she trespassed on sleep; but the head turned on the pillow, the eyes opened.

All in an instant the same considerations crowded on her for the hundredth time, to erode her with fear. Had her mother become bedfast merely in the order of nature, inexorable, or had it been brought on by some shock unadmitted or concealed? If so, how much risk was she taking in obliging a dying woman to recall it again, to speak of it? The thought undermined her with a sickness; at the same time, she had to know.

"Mummy," she said again. The face was turned toward her, waiting, the ivory face incised with the delicate sharp hieroglyph of a final advent, at the bridge of the nose and the jaw-line.

"Tell me," Auriol strove on. "Is anything . . . worrying you? I mean, is there anything on your mind?"

The incomprehension in Mrs. Chapman's eyes, the unreserve in her voice, sounded genuine.

"Why, no," she returned tranquilly. "Whatever put that in your mind, my love?"

"Well—nothing. I only thought," she laboured on, infelicitously, "if anything had worried you—or frightened you—"

"It's not likely that anything frightening could get at me." Mrs. Chapman smiled faintly. "Not here."

"Well then, I'm crackers. I only thought that if anything had happened that you hadn't told me about— anything unusual—"

"No, no. Except—" Into Mrs. Chapman's dismissiveness entered a belated qualification; nothing so important as an effort of memory, only a minor recollection. "—except—of course—those letters."

"What letters?" murmured Auriol. A cold void of consternation pierced her head and transfixed her body to more than a bird's stillness beneath the hawk's shadow.

"The first one startled me, of course," Mrs. Chapman was pursuing equably. "Even the second one, a little. After that I simply tore them up without opening them—I could tell them by then, you see." She smiled, again, her shadowy smile. "I wouldn't let you set eyes on anything like that, no fear."

Auriol swallowed, tried to say something, failed.

"Your father," the gentle voice, shaken with its malady, went on. "He once catalogued a collection of letters, I forget whose . . . Oh yes! Mr. Pitt's." Her reminiscence had turned to a sort of self-communion, at which she was smiling affectionately. "And it seemed it was a sort of hobby of Mr. Pitt's to save all the anonymous letters he received. Dreadful things, some of them— quite shocking." Her smile returned from the evocation of her husband to Auriol. "I do remember, though—"

"Mummy, don't think about it," Auriol interposed, able to speak and move again. "Anyway, you're talking too much."

"No I'm not—and I wanted to ask you." A new purpose of inquiry was in her face and voice. "I do remember that that first letter—it said I was giving you money for a divorce. Well, for a divorce or anything else—you and I know how much money I can give you, don't we?"

In her eye was a glint, amused yet questioning;

134

Auriol answered it with "Yes," and even, in response, smiled.

"You aren't getting a divorce, are you?" the fading voice went on.

"Of course not," Auriol lied roundly.

"I was certain of it. So you see . . ." Mrs. Chapman closed her eyes from the effort of talking; her voice fell lower. "Except for a moment, I wasn't frightened for you at all. And for myself—I can't be."

Seeming to wake again, she looked full at her daughter. In that look was a sudden concentrated essence of her spirit, and belatedly Auriol recognized it for what it was, having failed to recognize it in all these years of her existence. Indomitable, that was all; merely and simply, her mother was indomitable. And something even beyond, something more than indomitable, only what . . . ?

"How is Ivor?" Mrs. Chapman was saying.

"Very well," said Auriol. "Terribly busy."

"Oh, I know. And so good of him to let you spend so much time with me. Please"—her lips took on some of their old pretty shape when sending affectionate messages—"please give him my love."

"I will—I will, darling."

Some new thought seemed to rouse Mrs. Chapman from her half-sleep and arrest the impending descent of her heavy eyelids.

"It only just occurred to me," she said, looking surprised, "how unhappy, how frightfully unhappy a person must be—who needs to write letters like that."

"I expect," Auriol mumbled.

"Some poor twisted creature," pursued the failing voice. "They're not to blame very likely, not really."

This one's to blame, thought Auriol. A black hatred swirled in her head; for a moment she had the sensation of toppling. *This one, this one, this one's to blame.*

"Some poor, poor soul." As Mrs. Chapman closed her eyes and lay silent Auriol recognized, with a sort of shock, the ultimate quality of this frail life, fluttering on the verges of extinction, that she had failed to define earlier. Her mother was *safe*, safe in herself; safer than her daughter had ever been, or could be.

14

In Ivor's little house, lustrous with beauty, she had been nothing, and worse than nothing. Eroded with expensive emptiness and aimless days, awakening to her sluggard's existence where her chief occupation was to dress and perfume herself, she had been endlessly vulnerable, timidly propitiating, like a person waiting for some deserved blow to fall. In her mean rented flat, at once, she was no longer a creature obscurely pilloried, defeated, and apologetic. And in her small office at Stormonth's, at the battered desk piled with the work she knew how to do, her consequence was finally restored, and along with her consequence something else—or perhaps the two were synonymous: perhaps consequence, and safety, were the same thing.

It was that belated glimpse of her mother's inward spirit that had turned her, so frequently, to cogitating upon safety. To be safe: it was what every living creature wanted. But safety had many appearances, and when you took refuge in one or other of them, you could find it a spurious refuge. Marriage, for example: marriage was supposed to be safety, but that safety had evicted and betrayed her. Money was safety, but with Ivor's money all about her, she had never felt more naked or more exposed to peril. So in the end, perhaps, the only safety was work: the only citadel guaranteed safe from any assault but sickness and old age, and as yet she was healthy and far from old. And she was grateful, profoundly grateful, for the extra-heavy office pressures that had fallen on her directly after the funeral; it compelled her to turn her eyes from her own hurt and to concentrate all her forces on what waited, urgently, and could not be set aside or put off.

Actually her own small office, its physical features, was part of her feeling of security in these two late-Georgian houses side by side, inhabited by Stormonth's for one hundred and forty-two years. Originally good-class dwellings, they conformed to the usual pattern of such places: gloomy chopped-up ground floors, lofty noble first floors, and higher up a complicated warren of small rooms on different levels, joined by narrow passages of lunatic indirection and sudden outcrops of stairs in neck-breaking corners. Atop a longer flight of these, eight steps to be exact, her private and particular cell was perched like a tower room; she had always thought it might have held a big cistern in some bygone day. And with its character of isolation, of being high up and far away, it added its fortress-like safety to the other fortress she sheltered behind: the certainties of work and the certainties of her assumption—her rash and perilous assumption—that her abilities remained untouched and unscathed by the things that had happened to her and were still happening. Her very occasional moments of blackout were not worth noticing, and still less a darting pain in her eyes and temples; more and more frequent, yet hardly deserving to be dignified by the name of headache.

"How in hell did it happen?" The incredulity in her superior's voice, as he asked it for the third or fourth time, made it almost a plea rather than recrimination. "You—you of all people—to let a thing like this go through!"

Aghast, wordless, Auriol stared at the damning evidence of the page: the mistake that had slipped past her in galley-proof and that had given every reviewer in England, or publication, a field-day of savage derision.

"How?" he was imploring. "How? All right, it's up to the writer in the first instance, but in the second instance—that's why we employ a specializing editor, just to make doubly sure that things like this can't happen."

"Yes." Fumbling, she had found her voice if not the words to go with it. "It's—it's unpardonable. How anything so glaring got past me I—I don't know, Mark. I simply don't know."

"Neither do I." He was unappeased. "I know you've been having a hard passage, your mother and so forth. But still!" he expostulated. "But still!"

"Yes," she concurred, slow and dull, her gaze fastened upon the victim of her incapacity—the book, expensively produced, whose prospect of sales she had damaged irrecoverably. She could offer nothing but excuses, a commodity she had never dealt in; they were foreign to her nature. "My—my eyes, it might be my eyes," she groped lamely. "Glasses, perhaps . . . I see as well as ever but—I mean, I think I do," she corrected herself uncertainly. "But maybe . . . "

They sat in a lengthening silence, both of them darkened with an identical oppression; at the end of it he muttered, with conclusive disgust, "Well."

She took it for dismissal and started to rise.

"Just a moment," he interposed heavily. "One moment."

She sat down again, so swathed and muffled by humiliation that she was deaf to the new accent in his voice.

"This." He placed a ham-like hand on a pile of galleys before him, then picked up one and handed it over grimly. "Second par from the top."

As she read it, her eyes widening with horror and her mouth dropping open—

"Yes," he said savagely. "D'you realize we'd be fighting the libel suit of our lives, if this'd gone through?

139

D'you realize we'd be lucky to get off under ten or fifteen thousand quid?"

She produced a sound, less word than gasp.

"I don't know what put it in my head to look these things over after they'd left your hands," he drove on, "but thank Christ I did. All right, I caught it this time. But next time—?"

He let the implications drop between them and spread their widening circles.

"I depended on you," the arraignment went on. "I trusted you completely. But if I can't any more? If I daren't?"

He paused to let her answer, a purely token gesture; he knew there was no answer.

"And where's that leave us? If the work you've done has to be done over again by someone else, well then . . . ?" He spread his big hands, inviting the conclusion. "You see it yourself, don't you? How can we risk this sort of thing?" He dealt the pile of galleys, an indicative thump. "What publisher can afford it?"

A wavering took his voice, a new awkwardness, as the anger that had borne him up receded like a wave. "I'll tell you what, love," he said with false heartiness, "wouldn't you like a holiday?"

"A holiday?" she echoed vacantly, then sat up straighter; into the willing complicity of her self-abasement crept a vestige of wariness. "How long a holiday?"

"Well." He was uncomfortably jovial. "As long as you like. Make your husband take you away somewhere." He simpered archly. "A second honeymoon."

This might be reassurance that her personal affairs remained completely unknown at Stormonth, but the reassurance came a long way second to present and primary consideration.

"Mark," she appealed. Her voice must not betray her concern. "I'd so much rather you fired me outright, if you're doing it, than in this disguised way."

"Auriol," he appealed in turn. Under his discomfort was something inexorable; in all the years of their association she had never encountered this quality, and now saw it for what it was. He was unshakably genial; he was fond of her, presumably. But whatever his geniality and fondness, the rock-bottom truth was that he would get rid of anyone who complicated his life, and as quickly as possible.

"Auriol," he repeated his rare use of her entire first name, "What's the alternative? what else can I do?"

"Please," she managed. "It was a—a lapse, a momentary thing, it won't happen again. It won't—it won't, Mark."

"But what difference can it make to you—this job?" he asked, his real surprise responding to the timbre of desperation that had got away from her. "What possible difference?"

"It—it does. It does, Mark—I promise you."

He stared at her a long moment, then grunted; the fatally intelligent eyes in the fat face took on an approximate if not total comprehension, and in the same moment turned cold and rejecting. *Why d'you drag in your personal affairs?* they demanded. *What have they to do with this? I didn't ask to know about them.*

"Please," she continued her halting supplication. "Another—chance, if you'd give me one more chance. I'll be careful from now on, so careful. Please, Mark, please—!"

He grimaced at that last *please*, raw and shrill, then sat silent. Another pause intervened; at the end of it he shrugged, scowled, and said, "Well." No longer looking at her he chewed the cud of some reflection that gave his lips a look of distaste. She had bludgeoned him into this reprieve against his better judgment, on a basis emotional and not professional; it was something he would hold against her. Finally he swivelled his chair abruptly and presented his back to her. Over his shoulder he threw, "For God's sake, girl, pull up your socks." His voice was without humour, surly and dismissive.

The silence that fell upon Stormonth's after working hours, a vacuum of silence, was only an extension of the vacuum she confronted as she sat alone in her office; except that this vacuum, personal and private to herself, happened to be her future. Into it she stared and could see only one thing: her own destruction. And if it sounded overdone, even hysterical, she could find nothing wrong with her diagnosis on more dispassionate scrutiny. Her mother was no longer an avenue by which she could be attacked and injured, but there were other avenues. Yet, for a person so attacked, somewhere there must be protection . . .

She started thinking about protection. The law? but she had appealed there, and found out about the law. Huge in its mass, huge also in its deficiency; whole yet amputated, active yet passive, powerful yet powerless. If Ivor were to shoot, stab, or poison her, the law in all its panoply would move to her aid—when aid could be to her of less than no interest. But he could surround her with impalpable menaces and torments, and so long as he managed it cleverly enough he stood beyond the law, out of reach. He could distort every aspect of her existence, he could destroy her . . .

With a shrug, she made the essential correction. He *had* destroyed her; he had set out to do it, and he had done it. He had filled her life as a daughter with anxieties and terrors, he had driven Maggie and Tom away from her and would make it his business to molest or intimidate, similarly, anyone whose relationship with her was conspicuous enough to draw his attention. Now, having shut her into a void of friendlessness, with the same lethal rot he was eating away her ultimate fortress, her work.

And quietly, all of it done so quietly. Destruction need not be a noisy shattering thing, it could be as deathly quiet as this. She remembered a river starting to flood the valley where they holidayed once; just before the wholesale evacuation of the area, she had gone out once more and seen the water coming up soundlessly, with hardly a ripple in its surface; silent annihilation, utterly silent.

She began reviewing means of escape. If her nerves, concentration, and memory were so eroded that she could no longer be useful to a publisher, what could she do? Well, look for a teaching job; in some small school, withering from day to day in the wrong profession, she could lie buried and safe, as people in graves were safe. Or run away? emigrate? But she was English, her roots were in England, she had no thought of being driven out of it to settle in another land, and never had had, yet to this thought also he was coercing her . . .

A wild flare of hatred and rebellion took her, in the same moment that she recognized herself as impotent. Revenge herself on Ivor, how? Did people of her kind have recourse to guns, knives, poison? Ludicrous. What had been bred and implanted in her from infancy was fatal to such savageries; fatal to her very instinct of self-preservation in that she had rather be—in all cases—the cheated rather than the cheater, the spoiled than the spoiler, the slain than the slayer. The name of this infection that weakened her so fatally was civilization, merely civilization. Yet even this Ivor had been able to invade, goading her into degrading frenzies where she shouted and screamed at him in a voice unrecognizable to herself, disgusting . . .

Finally, the empty wastes that she surveyed presented her with one more emptiness. The divorce: she had been counting on the divorce, living for it literally, as the answer to all her problems. But from her high and lonely crow's-nest, she saw it answered nothing. Having it would not prevent his gadfly persecutions, if he chose to follow them up; she might still be in the same position, ousted from one refuge and scrabbling for another, always fleeing his malignity, always the hunted animal . . .

When she heard the footsteps at last, they could no longer be very far off. The first floor was opulently carpeted, every inch of it, but up here all halls and stairs were naked wood, except her own eight steps which were slate, with an iron hand-rail. Startled suddenly out of arid brain-racking, incredulous at first, she listened. The sounds had the peculiar sharpness of all sound in an empty building, a distant echoing resonance, but unmistakably approaching. A prowler? a burglar? Tucked away up here she was probably out of his route, yet if she called the police he might be drawn by the vague impinging of her voice, however low, upon the silence . . . at this instant the footsteps changed in character, walking on wood no longer, but on stone. He was on her staircase; her closed door had misled her as to his actual nearness. Belatedly she realized what a magnet her light must have been, blasting out through the ribbed glass in the upper half of her door and casting its halation down the steps and into the dark passage. He was coming up at a peculiar gait, either hesitant or ominously slow. Now three steps separated them, now two, now one . . . bound by fear and a lethal paralyzing curiosity she heard the hand on the knob, saw it turn, saw the opening door and the head appear through it . . .

Startled equally, gaping equally, she and Tom stared at each other. After a moment—

"I thought—" they said in unison, then laughed in unison; both shaky, she with relief, he with relief and awkwardness in solution.

"Good Lord," he achieved utterance first. "I could see this vague reflection of light all the way from outside my door, and I couldn't think what it was."

"I know," she apologized. "Naturally you'd investigate," seeing meanwhile the initial amiability fade from his face and annoyance replace it. *He'd rather have found an intruder here,* a corner of her mind commented; then, even more irrelevantly, *His love-affair's still going badly; he's grim, but grimness is becoming to him.*

"What a damned-fool trick this is," he accused irritably, "your working alone in this empty barracks. Suppose I'd been someone else? You could've screamed blue murder and nobody'd hear you."

"But it wasn't someone else," she summoned a foolish flippancy. "It was you."

He frowned; her retort had failed to please.

"Come on, Roly," he said peremptorily. "Pack it up. Come on, get the hell out and go home."

The spurious affability faded from her face in turn, leaving it expressionless.

"Tom," she said in a measured voice, "go away."

A blank moment took over, a space of time during which his surprise at her tone was evident, also his unpreparedness; he had never heard anything like it from her.

"I'm not trying to take charge—" he began awkwardly.

"You were," she cut him off. "You were doing just that. Well, I mayn't be here much longer, but while I am, let me alone, will you?" Her voice was controlled and much too deliberate. "Just let me alone, it's all I ask."

He stood his ground; into his face came a faint disturbance of inquiry.

"Go away," she pursued. "Just please go away."

"How's that?" he asked, ignoring the dismissal. "What do you mean, you mayn't be here much longer?" He waited some moments, then hazarded, "You've made it up, then? you're going back to Ivor?"

"No, I am not going back to Ivor," she retorted. "I'm going to my reserved seat on the Embankment."

During another pause, a saturnine amusement came into his face; the picture of Auriol among the London homeless evidently failed to carry conviction.

"Come on," he rallied her; a gentleness had come into his tone, something of the old Tom. "But don't tell me Mark had anything to do with your leaving, because I won't believe it."

"I don't care whether you believe it or not." That she

145

could speak without her voice turning ragged heartened her immensely; she was going to get through this exchange without the shame of breaking down. "It's not of the least importance."

"But he knows he can't get anybody to touch you," Tom expostulated. "My God, when you left he held you up to all your miserable successors like a heavenly example or something."

"Perhaps he did—then."

"Then—?"

"In the last two weeks," she explained evenly, "I've made two boos of the first magnitude—"

"You?"

"No one else." Her stony face and harsh voice repelled his interruption and his incredulity. "One's going to cost us a lot of money, the other was caught in time, thank God—by Mark. But you see his position? How can he rely on me any more? Oh, he was kind about it, he didn't try just to throw me out, nothing like that. He said why didn't I go off on a nice trip somewhere with —with my husband—"

Something began bubbling up in her like an unclean ferment, a horrible mirth, racking and resistless—

"—a h-honeymoon, he s-said," she hiccoughed, giggling. "A s-s-second honeymoon—"

She put her elbows on the desk and her face into her hands and began to laugh, peal after peal. From far off she heard his alarmed "Roly!" and at the same time her merriment turn loud then violent, then the crazy laughter to sobs, the sobs to screams . . . In the grip of a first-class bout of hysterics, she was desperately ashamed at the same time; ashamed of the horrid sounds she was letting loose, that in the small bare room echoed back on her ears with an added indecency. Obliterated by paroxysm she had lost all sense of Tom, his disappearance, his reappearance . . .

"Here." He had pushed her back in her chair, brusquely put his palm under her chin and raised her head, and was holding something to her lips. "Come on, drink this. Just a sip, come on. Come on, knock it back, good girl, that's right, come on—"

It was water, into which he had dumped enough aromatic spirits to make her choke on the first swallow, then cough, gasp, and push the glass away. Yet better to be strangling and fighting to recover than be as she had been a moment before, sub-human and chaotic with outcry, and she was grateful; grateful to be emerging, to be sane once more . . .

"I'm—sorry," she managed. "S-sorry, Tom, so—"

"Shut up," he said harshly. He was busying himself with something, she could hear a slight splash of water on the floor, then he had lifted her head again and begun mopping at her face. She sat vacant and passive as an infant, sometimes sighing gustily, while his handkerchief, too wet, passed and repassed and shed big trickles down her neck. Wonderful, the cool damp cloth on her forehead and eyelids, wonderful, a blessing. And the hand that moved it, the man so big and powerful and the hand clumsy, yet the gentleness, the *gentleness* . . .

"There." He was surveying the scene of his operations. "Feel better?"

"Oh yes, much. Oh Tom, I *am* sorry." She tried to sit straighter. "I'm all right now."

"You're fine," he said grimly. "Never seen you better, At the top of your form, you are."

"No, no, it was—it was just a—I'm sorry I've kept you here for nothing, but you go along now, I'm absolutely all right. Oh Lord, I must look a wreck." She brushed futilely at her hair. "You run along, Tom. And thank you, darling, thank you—"

"Quit thanking me, for Christ's sake." Scraping chair-legs made a raw gash on the silence as he pulled up a seat and planted himself in it. "Now tell me about it, come on. Come on, Roly, tell me."

Both were silent for some moments after she had finished talking. Cancelled by fatigue as she was, stupid

147

and drained, she was yet aware, with a muzzy surprise, of relief; even to have shared with someone else what she had been carrying alone, was a sort of comfort. Delusive, it could make no real difference to her trouble, yet how kind of him to listen, how kind . . .

"Yes," he said finally, his gaze inbent; he was not talking to her. "Yes."

"And don't you see?" she exposed the final, ruinous codicil. "Whether I'm divorced or not, what's to prevent his going on with these things he's doing to me, and anything new he can think of? And I've tried to get help, I told you—there is no help."

"Mh'm," he grunted, as far away as before.

"A private detective?" she beat along the spiny trail she had beaten a thousand times before. "At five or ten pounds a day? And if he suspects he's followed he'll break off for a month, then begin again. Who can keep up with a thing like that? Don't you see?" she implored. "Divorce or no divorce, he can make my life a nightmare. They can't catch him either, he's too clever, he can do what he likes. And he will, too," she ended wildly. "He will, he will—!"

Again there was a long stillness in the room during which, like an earthquake survivor in the wreckage of her home, she sat with sagging shoulders, with staring appalled eyes and open mouth . . . Emerging after some unmeasured interval she looked at her companion, still engrossed with the image of her disaster and hardly seeing him. It took another moment before she woke up: first to his silence which had been different from her silence, then to his look, still absorbed—as hers had been —in some inward, ungrateful vision. And whatever this vision was, it had carved his face to a mask, a dark baleful mask with hooded eyes. As this dawned on her he raised his head, his gaze coming to rest on her but still (she knew) not seeing her.

"What I like about this," he observed softly and pleasantly, "was his being able to scare me away from you with his spying and his dirty little threats, and send me scuttling for my crack." He spoke only half to her, and perhaps not at all. "I like thinking of that—it makes me feel good. He cracked the whip, and I jumped." His smile did not lighten his face, but darkened it; a disquieting effect. "I thank him for that. I owe him something for that."

Somehow not daring to interrupt the soliloquy of the unknown who had replaced Tom, the hard ruthless stranger, she gaped almost without recognition; in that moment he got up abruptly, and was aware of her again.

"Let me think about this," he said. "We'll talk again tomorrow night. Not at your flat," he stipulated. "It may be one of the times he's watching you. Here's best then, I expect? between seven and eight?" Seeming barely to look at her he commanded, "And run along now, don't argue. I'd take you home, but perhaps better not. I'll stop here awhile—you go first."

"This telephone thing," he began without preamble, and digressed suddenly, "did it ring last night?"

"Twice," she nodded.

"And this happens when, you said—?"

"Between three and four seems to be the—the witching hour." She smiled painfully. "Seldom earlier, and never later."

"It's a pattern then. To that extent," he qualified. "Now let me ask the questions." His glance exacted obedience. "All right, you say there's a sort of regularity about the time. Now." His eyes took renewed hold of her. "Is there anything else about it that's regular? Anything at all that consistent, invariable—?"

"Rainy nights seem to bring it on." She had been going to omit this grotesqueness as improbable; a shiver traversed her as she said it. "Rain sets it off. I thought at first it was my imagination, but it wasn't."

"He knows the value of a stage setting." His voice

went brittle; he smiled. "Sensitive bloke. All right, and once he begins it, how long does he keep it up?"

"That's what's so . . . erratic. But one thing I *have* noticed." Uncertainly, in the cobweb haze, she groped for the vague outline. "If it happens two nights in succession, it's likely to go on five or six nights. It's doing that now."

"And last night was what, of this series—?"

"The"—she had to think—"the fourth, I expect."

"It's running out to an end then, this time?"

She nodded.

"Well, we'll get ready for next time. 'It'll take us awhile to rig it, anyway." With a movement of his hand he cut off her attempt to speak. "Now look: I want you to do what I tell you. Apply for a phone extension." His voice was peremptory. "Have it in the same room or the next room, so long as it's in sight of the other phone. I know someone in Postal Telephones," he subjoined. "You'll get it pretty well at once."

"I'll do it—straightaway."

"Good. Now also at once, I want you to arrange with some friend to stop with you nights, as soon as the calls begin again. Have you anyone that close—anyone you can trust to that extent?"

"I don't know." *It would have been easy once, but not now.* "Actually, no. No, I haven't."

"Well, put your mind to it—see if you can dig up someone."

"I will," *Putting my mind to it won't dig me up a friend like that.*

"At the worst," he was saying, "we'll bring in a professional. Now"—he paused an instant; his glance, a spear, transfixed hers—"now here's the drill for the next lot of calls. As soon as the phone rings, both of you pick up, the other person at the extension, *but*—only you answer. Only you, get it? The other one just listens. You'll be up till the small hours," he predicted. "It's a nuisance, but it's the only way I can think of, to pin this thing."

150

"Yes." Her submissiveness was invaded by a half-comprehension, chilling.

"O.K. Now when you've answered, and nobody's there, don't ring off. Hang on long enough for me to come on the line and speak to you. That's how it'll be, if we bring it off—I'll speak to you."

"Yes," she muttered, though he was so rapt in calculation that no answer was necessary. "Yes."

"Of course"—moodily he was soliloquizing—"if I go for him, and make a mess of it—"

The half-formed picture turned her cold again.

"—then," Tom pursued, "then of course we've had it. He'll be warned off this particular amusement, and turn his talents to something else. However"—he straightened—"we can only try. So after you've both answered, remember—hang on at least a couple of minutes. If I haven't come on by then, give it up."

She nodded, seeing him always unaware of her; his eyes were preoccupied, his uncertainties wrapped him thickly in gloom.

"Something tells me," he communed with himself, "that either we bring it off the first time, or not at all."

Still warmed by the thought of an ally, but intimidated by his unvoiced doubts, she muttered, hangdog, "Thank you."

"One chance." He had not even heard her. "Pure hairline. How do I know I won't muck it? Can't. Can't know."

"Why in God's name"—her voice broke slightly—"you should trouble—"

His eyes—hard eyes—saw her now; his mouth softened. "Don't talk balls, darling. It's a change from print rooms in museums."

Something awoke in his face, and vanished quickly. Only much later, seeing it in retrospect—the curious flash, dark and grim—did she identify it for what it was: pure pleasure.

Just before mounting the four stone steps to her front door she paused an instant, looking quickly right and left and thinking, *What if he's somewhere nearby, what if he's watching again,* then regretted the quick apprehensive movement of her head; if he had seen it he would know what it meant, and be amused. The street at this moment had its normally lifeless look, especially after nightfall, and also seemed unfavourable for concealment. Still, that meant nothing; when she had let Tom out and called good night to him the usual emptiness had seemed to prevail everywhere, yet he had been lurking nearby. Withdrawn into one of the long dark row of porticos, or into the hedge of the square garden opposite, where it was deeply cut back for the gates; unseen and unsuspected he had been somewhere, somewhere . . .

The vision of herself dogged always, observed always, slowed her as she climbed the stairs to her flat; the deathly quiet of the hallways, their faint mustiness, seemed a sort of refuge. As she inserted her key and opened the door, her phone was ringing.

It was the measure of her disintegration that a prosaic convenience had assumed for her the very voice and shape of evil; that she was, literally, afraid to answer. Rooted where she had entered, she stood gaping and conjecturing. Beside Tom, who must be able to reach her, no person had this number. From her, or on her mother's behalf, there would be no more calls. Improbable that Tom himself was ringing, since she had just parted from him. Let it blast away, presently it must stop . . .

It did anything but stop; the small black mound, shrilling and shrilling beyond any degree of sane persistence, was in itself an advertisement of malice, some new malice. Better find out what it was, better now than three o'clock in the morning . . . Violently she choked off its clamour, picking it up and half-shouting into it, "Hello!"

The expected, mocking silence met her; just about to

repeat her challenge, she was stopped by a voice saying, "Well, thank God."

From mere shock, she was silent.

"It didn't sound like you," said the phone. "Shook me for a moment. I was going to reach you if it took all day and all night."

"How—" Auriol swallowed; one of the foolish inapposite questions born of stress came, uninvited. "How did you get this number?"

"Getting ex-directory numbers? in my business?" A dark unamusement tinged Maggie's voice. "Don't be naive. The question is, will you speak to me?"

"I seem to be doing," said Auriol. "Speaking to you."

"Cheeky as usual," said Maggie. "And believe me, I'm grateful to you. If you'd like to wipe your boots on me, I'll still be grateful."

"I—I don't want to wipe my boots on you."

"Look." Maggie's tone discarded inessentials. "I feel as though I'd been under a drug or something, and just come out of it. What in hell ailed me, that I let that queer do that to me? That I let myself be intimidated— cowed—by that poisonous little rat? What was the matter with me? Was I crackers, or what?"

"The shock." Auriol rushed to make it easier for her. "Having it thrown at you like that—"

"Shock, ——," Maggie cut her off with one of her fruitier expletives. "I've handled uglier customers than Hailes, and I let him scare me witless all the same. I can't bear it, I tell you. As if I weren't equal to the worst he could think up! Christ Jesus, I keep wanting to spit in my own face."

"I didn't blame you. I never blamed—"

"You poor stupid donkey," Maggie interrupted, with a sort of ferocious patience. "Your blaming me or not blaming me is the least of it. The one important thing is, I must be able to live with myself without vomiting. Auriol, listen"—her scalding self-contempt changed to petition—"anything I can do for you, just ask me. As a favour," she specified. "Just ask me at any time.

Or—now?" she demanded in sudden afterthought. "Now? Is there anything I can do?"

"Maggie." Behind Auriol's supplication lurked a wry, bitter-sweet amusement. Maggie and Tom, leaving her and coming back to her, both in almost-identical terms; impinging echoes of rejection and loss, impinging echoes of renewal and restoration, like a pre-arranged effect . . .

"Yes? What?" Maggie had snapped like a starving trout at the mere nuance of entreaty; it might have been worth a smile at any other time.

"Well, there *is* something—or there will be something—"

"What? what?"

"I don't quite know yet. I mean, I haven't been told everything. Actually, I shouldn't involve you—"

"Shut up. Go on," Maggie commanded inconsistently, "with what you were saying."

"Well, I can't give you details till I have them myself. I only know," Auriol warned, "that it can't be nice, it's bound to be unpleasant—"

"Tell me as far as you can," Maggie broke in again. "Tell me."

15

How much the job was a matter of surveillance had been evident from the beginning, but not how much a matter of luck. In what proportion, he realized only belatedly; without luck on top of the surveillance, whatever he did would be useless. In the meantime and during these preliminary stages, he was limited to reconnoitering; smelling out the lay of the land as thoroughly as possible.

From the first of these nocturnal expeditions, his life changed its whole shape and form. From nine in the evening he slept, partly dressed; an alarm-clock woke him at one. He put on some disreputable clothes reserved for the country, a bulky sagging jersey, a pair of comfortable shoes, rubber-soled, then got his car and steered for SWI. He parked with utmost ease in the broad silent street where quiet prevailed, the special quiet of residential areas where rents are £1200 a year upward. The mews, which he did not know at all, was somewhere near. Padding along, peering at street signs, he found it at last, then located the house, its expensive charm evident even in this unlight, fog-tainted, that bleached away whatever colour it was painted. After the house came the question of the observation-post, and here things were not favourable. The mews, cobbled its whole length, very broad and especially well-kept—it must be part of the ducal estate that owned vast stretches of the neighbourhood—was poor as could be for purposes of concealment. He scouted silently and cautiously from end to end, wondering what figure he would present to the eyes of a patrolling cop, and finally had to settle for nothing better than a doorway two houses down on the same side; much too shallow but not so shallow as its neighbours, and also flanked by two ornamental trees in tubs. These were a Godsend, also he would have to count on the rather poor lighting of the mews—subdued, no doubt, by preference of the tenants. This much done, he slunk up the cobbled-way again to the immensely broad thoroughfare planted with gardens down its middle, where again the silence of the grave prevailed. No cop or other living soul, thank God, not even a passing car, near as they were to Belgrave Square.

Now it remained to pin-point, if he could, the call-boxes most obviously and immediately contiguous for Ivor's use, in this old neighbourhood of unexpected corners and niches; he had to be familiar with their locations, especially on these late November nights; the vile obscured nights of coming winter, when the pursuer might easily lose track of the pursued. It might take him more than one evening, he thought, to find all the kiosks within a sufficient radius. Well, that was all right; the caller lay quiescent between bouts and the last of them was just over, so he should have plenty of time for his researches. Methodically he tunnelled the neighbourhood in widening circles, an assiduous maggot in foggy cheese, triumphant whenever he spotted one of his objectives, like a big dim lantern sitting on the ground. They seemed mainly to lurk in the shadow of the huge old archways that constituted the entrance to ancient rows of stables, sometimes culs-de-sac and sometimes not, long converted to dwellings, garages and other uses.

Then it occurred to him, with sudden misgiving: what if Ivor used his car to attain some call-box more distant from his house? The thought was undermining, but only for a moment. To get a car out in the small hours was a comparatively noisy process; infinitely more silent, more discreet, to walk. The idea of other transportation he dismissed at once, even having to smile at the picture of the elegant Hailes on a scooter or bicycle.

And this was enough for a first expedition, he was bone-tired, aching in every limb and suddenly aware of the alien, disowning quality that inhabits all darkness. He liked his share of night-life but this was another kind, and a small spiteful rain powdered disagreeably on his face, driven by an intermittent wind. Poor Roly, frightened by the coincidence of rain and the phone calls, to which she attached a sinister significance; of course the little rat would choose nights when bad weather emptied the streets and made visibility poorest, there was no more to it than that. Or on second thought, perhaps there was something more . . . All at once, grotesquely, he remembered Zola's prostitute; the girl who—hardened to her calling and by no means nervous about it—maintained that rain brought a special kind of man out into the streets, and was always afraid of the clientele she picked up on rainy nights.

"It's a miserable couch," said Auriol. "If only you'd take my bed—"

"It's nothing," said Maggie. "Don't natter."

"Well"—Auriol's voice all at once bit the silence, unrecognizably corrosive—"you can thank dear Ivor for the pleasure of staying up all night on bumps and springs, instead of sleeping in your own lovely bed."

There followed an interval for which she seemed unprepared, having expected reinforcements to her invective; she looked up inquiringly. But Maggie sat quiet, with lowered eyelids, her face desolate and still.

"Yes," she muttered at last, unresponding. "What time is it?" She looked. "Isn't your lad overdue? Anyway, I shouldn't have left my station." She began to get out of her chair, always an unwieldy process. "It's after four—from now on let's stick by our guns."

"Don't bother." Auriol's tone, leaden, was a legitimate offspring of her raw misery of secret knowledge; it was too terrible, she had to share it with someone. "He's failed, Tom's failed—already."

"How d'you make that out?" But Maggie's demand was hushed with consternation. "How can you know?"

"Because he—he told me—he'd have to bring it off the first time, or not at all. And that one—Ivor—he always rings by now, if he's going to. So it means—he knows he was watched. And Tom knows, too—that he was spotted, and he doesn't want to tell me. He doesn't want to tell me he's failed." Her tone withered to lifelessness. "He was going to follow, he couldn't have done any differently, and of course he was seen. Ivor"—the name twisted her mouth for an instant—"wouldn't be caught by anything so transparent." She sighed. "Think of being hated that much, by a man that warped." She sighed again, sounding querulous and old. "Like some infection. All around you."

Maggie stood wordless and unaggressive; she too looked older, and helpless.

"I'd get you some tea, but . . . but let's not give up quite yet," she said finally. "Let's keep it up a bit, you never know." She vanished into the other room, where, sitting at the phones, she and Auriol were in each other's line of vision.

"It's well on four," said Maggie, from the doorway. "Has he ever rung this late?"

"Never." She was dull, dishevelled from fighting sleep.

"He won't call now, you think?"

"No," murmured Auriol. "No, he won't call now." Her voice seemed to come from a trance, somnambulistic. "He'll think of something else. He'll do something else."

The door opened so silently that he heard nothing at all from his distance of only a few yards away, though he had been waiting for the sound. Putting his head out cautiously from the doorway and peering beneath the right-hand tree, he saw the figure emerge, with—its emergence completed—again no sound from the door. The silhouette, black against the dim light, began moving toward the head of the mews; even at this distance its litheness and grace were perceptible. Apparently rubber-shod, he moved with swift and noiseless purpose and with a gait somehow reminiscent of a ballet dancer's. Tom, coming out of ambush and following at the greatest possible distance, was rent by a variety of apprehensions: first of letting him get too far away, for the instant he turned right or left at the top of the mews he would be out of sight; second, by the task he had taken on—of dogging a man superior to himself in intelligence and acuteness of faculty, and moreover a man preternaturally alert because of his discreditable mission. Stoutly repressing a cold premonition of failure, and quickening his pace—for the quarry was almost out of the mews—he was struck again by the lissome swaying quality of the other's gait. Aside from their first infelicitous encounter, Tom had seen him once or twice escorting Auriol, and had no recollection at all of this undulant walk; in the public eye, and in correct masculine clothes, presumably he controlled it. His pursuer's face, in the darkness, was flicked by an additional malice and distaste; his vengefulness of intent quickened. With this needle of scorn in him, he was no longer so convinced of the inevitability of failure. And he must run, the dark figure had turned left and out of sight; if he slipped on the treacherous cobbles, the thud of his weight coming down could not go unheard in these sleeping silences, even from that far off perhaps . . . His burst of speed, trammelled by caution, left him upright; at a distance the other was passing through a wan pool of street light, melting into shadow beyond its radius. A brief reassurance possessed the hunter; thanks to his researches in the neighbourhood, he was fairly certain of the other's destination. His surmise proved correct, and still lurking at a considerable distance, he saw the man go toward a kiosk that stood just outside a mews, no dwellings in this one but only the rear of a long row of shops giving on it; shabby and rank-smelling like most of that ilk, and of a black, utter desertion. As the figure entered the capsule of light it solidified suddenly into clearer outline chopped by latticed squares; within this enclosure its movements were vague, like those of a partly obscured reptile in a tank, and there burst on Tom, watching, the virtual impossibility of what he proposed to do. To approach with sufficient stealth, to pluck open the door with lightning speed—those doors were heavy and moved resistingly—to snatch the phone from the caller's hand, for if he had time to ring off the whole thing went bust . . . Already in despair yet moving indecisively forward, half-cogitating, half-readying himself, he saw within the box a ringing-off motion, too sudden for any call to have been put through; saw the man turn, push the door open, come out with a curious sort of haste . . .

Paralyzed with emergency, his own dismay obscuring the character of the other's movements, yet he managed to keep moving forward, to go past Hailes and continue on down the mews. It was an unlikely destination except for someone bent on mischief, that narrow stretch blinded with iron shutters or padlocked garage doors all along both sides, but there was no place else to go. Moving through the dustbin taint and scatter of trash underfoot, he wondered if the worst had not already happened, if he had not already botched the enterprise beyond repair. He had been seen, indubitably. But Hailes's sudden irruption from the box, did it mean alarm or something much more fatal—recognition? With his eyes accustomed by now to the obscure light, with his every fibre of alertness strung tight, how could he help but know the man who had passed him only a couple of yards away? And bareheaded; the most thick-witted

160

fool would have worn a cap. Tormenting himself with surmise, berating himself savagely he plodded out of the mews and toward his car, his heart and heels equally heavy with sickness of failure.

The answer, if he had known it, was almost amusing; a simultaneous awareness, on both sides, of baleful possibilities not previously envisaged. Ivor's precipitate emergence from the call-box had been instinctive, but the instinct was pure alarm and nothing else. On his many similar excursions he had met hardly a living soul; now all at once in the utter silence and desertion, glancing behind him, he saw a hulking shabby silhouette coming straight toward the kiosk, and understandably the image that leaped to his mind was of robbery with violence. Rather than be pinned in the box he had come out, but already he felt the cosh about his head and shoulders and knew he had no chance, not a chance in the world; the man looked big and powerful through the dimness and the half-rain, a brute, he might have a knife on him, a gun, anything . . .

His emotion therefore, when the menace slunk on past him and down the mews, was of overwhelming relief; easing his tightened chest with an exhalation, he took time for nothing but to get away quickly. The likelihood of a thug's assault had not occurred to him at all, and the presence he had seen could be up to no good making for the deserted mews, whose commercial character was perfectly well known to him. Long after he had got safely home the disruption of the episode, profound and disagreeable, was enough to put him in two minds about tomorrow night's prowl. While balancing indecisions, next morning, he combed the papers for mention of a robbery in any of the shops backing on the mews, and was obscurely disappointed not to find it.

If the tocsin had triggered off these various alarms for Ivor, its clamour in Tom's ears was no less strident, though on counts quite dissimilar. Only now for the first time he saw the deadly peril of his position should the ambush, during any stage of its progress, be observed.

His lurking in the mews, solitary; his silent following of Hailes; all of it must look fairly sinister. And then the climax, if he could bring it off: the two struggling bodies pent in the dim glass box, the appearance of murderous attack . . . his head swam as he realized what he might have let himself in for—given any passing spectator or policeman—and it would be his unsupported word against Hailes's. The whole look of the thing would stink to high heaven . . .

Suddenly the fiasco he was cursing appeared in the light of salvation—deliverance. *Someone with me from tomorrow night on,* he thought, unlocking the car. A *witness*, in case, and was glad he knew such a witness.

16

"It's no use," he said, barely achieving a whisper. The movement of his companion's head toward him signified that he had been heard, but no response was offered; both waited for something further. Another interval elapsed while the two men, pressed into the doorway scarcely deep or wide enough for one, listened to the silence; to the air-stirred leaves of their sheltering trees, to their own breathing. Far off a vague ribbon of sound slurred across the stillness, car tyres on a street somewhere, then again nothing.

"Nearly four," Tom mouthed near the other's ear, and as if in agreement a church clock began to strike, its bell so purged of tone by distance and night as to be a mere beating on the air, a remote unresonant pulse. "Come on, let's pack it up." Remarkable, how the scarcely breathed words could convey such a snarl of anger and disgust, and without further exchange they started up the mews; near the top, Tom touched his companion's sleeve and they halted, listening.

"I haven't met a cop so far and I don't want to," he murmured. "It's all I need. Still, they don't walk all that quietly." In a thick silence they continued padding toward their car, in silence drove toward their first port of call. Here they sat for moments, still wordless, till Tom breached the long interval with, "Well, he won't be coming out again. I mucked it last night—fouled the whole thing straightaway." Each syllable, thick with defeat, fell like a stone. "Let him lay eyes on me the very first time—Christ, what a fumbler, what a clot! Well"— he exhaled from a leaden breast—"we've had it."

"Oh, I don't know," said the other, after a moment. "Maybe he couldn't see you all that well."

"Couldn't see me! but how could he help—"

"Look, at that time of night, and someone coming upon you unexpectedly—you'd be too rattled, or too scared, to recognize your daddy. With this bloke, the chances are he was thinking of a cosh."

"But I was facing him directly," Tom argued. "Facing him and walking toward him."

"If you were walking toward the archway, the street light must have been behind you. All he probably saw was the big ugly size of you." He grinned; in the darkness his teeth gleamed extraordinarily white. "I'd hate to see anything of your dimensions bearing down on me in an empty street, at three in the morning. In that light, too, I expect you'd show up twice as big as you are."

"You may have something there." Tom revived uncertainly. "Yes, perhaps you've got something. Well, would you try it just once again, tomorrow night?"

"No," said his friend. "We run it for a week, or not at all. You don't footle with a thing like this, you do it or you don't do it."

"Thank you." His voice, quickened, was eloquent of the burden lifting from his heart. "Thanks, Michael."

"Oh, I like it," the other disclaimed, in his unchanging tone of reasonableness. "Anyway, I've a family interest in the matter." The flash of teeth could be half-seen again in the darkness. "He's played fast and loose with Postal Telephones' fair name. "He's—he's—"

"—put the damsel to vile and unseemly uses," Tom helped his dwindling stock of metaphor. "All right, get to hell out of this and let me go home, will you? Better get what sleep we can."

"Right." Michael, opening the door, turned. "The

next couple of times should tell us, at least, whether you've frightened him off permanently or only for the time being. Good night!"

"Good morning," Tom corrected sourly. In his mind, as he drove away, the image of their useless waiting kept pace with the image of Auriol's useless waiting; she and her friend, glued to the phones . . .

Of yet a second image—a night-after-night succession of other fruitless vigils for all of them—he preferred not to let himself think.

The two men exchanged a quick glance in darkness, the gesture sensed rather than seen by each one. Then again, scarcely breathing, they stole what unhandy glances they could at the shadow that emerged soundlessly from its door. The obscurity that fought against them had a peculiar muffled quality, thick weather beneath a dirty blanket of sky, veiled with drizzle and inhabited moreover with a bone-piercing chill. Not for the first time Tom marvelled at the depth of hatred that could pluck a man out of his warm luxurious home and drive him abroad into the cold and wet, for the commission of sub-human lunacies such as these . . . Meanwhile he had stepped urgently from concealment, when an imperative tug at his sleeve halted him.

"It's no good," Michael said under his breath. "You'll never catch him tonight. Look at him."

Tom looked. The quarry, approaching the head of the mews, was fairly distinct against the street lighting beyond, and now he perceived what Michael had seen and what he himself, oblivious of all but the chase, had failed to see. The man was pursuing his way without hesitation, yet with a tight mistrust in every step, and as he advanced his head jerked watchfully, now to this side and now to that. Even at that distance, wariness and suspicion emanated from him like an acrid odour; as Tom's senses picked it up, the other spoke again.

"He smells a rat," he murmured. "Night before last put him on his guard, you see? He's doing a test run tonight." He chuckled. "Let him pick up a hint that he's followed, the least hint, and he'll never come out again, and then you've had it."

"I know." He started moving as he said it. "Come on."

"But you can't jump him tonight, I tell you. He's too ready, he's alert—"

"I want to see what he does."

"But look, if he spots us—"

"He won't. For Christ's sake come *on*, he's gone around the corner—!"

Soundlessly they loped up the mews; peering left, they saw the man-shaped darkness melting into the other darkness. The visible caution that trammelled him made his progress slower than usual, else they must have lost him. As they strained their eyes after him, he turned left again.

"It's all right," said Tom. From sheer relief, he spoke in almost a natural tone. "I know the call-box he's going to."

Walking hard, almost running, they reached the corner.

"There's no call-box," Michael accused, hoarse from mere tension.

"The pub," hissed Tom. "There's a pub with a fore-court, and it's in there."

"We can't go right up and watch him," his ally pointed out.

"No need—just to see where he's been. There's shrubbery in boxes all along it—see?"

"I see. Look," Michael complained urgently, "this street's too damned well lighted."

"Get behind there, quick—I'll stand here."

There and *here* were massive gate-posts of long-vanished Victorian carriage-sweeps, such as one sees on Craven Hill; apparently too formidable to knock down, a long row of them had been left, portentous sentries to box-like modern flats, whose flimsiness they shamed. Sheltering behind these monoliths none too soon, they

166

saw the object of pursuit come out where a low ragged line marked the hedge. Again, on emergence, his circumspection was evident; he stood a full twenty seconds or so looking in every direction, especially along the path he had come, which had a slight downhill pitch. Then, apparently reassured, he started retracing his steps in a fashion which could only be called jaunty. As he swung along past them he came full into the light of a street lamp, and Tom saw his face.

A couple of years ago, visiting friends in Pennsylvania, he had encountered what the English have no conception of—the lethal oppressions of the American summer; the murdering humidity, the stifling heat that made his very pillow and mattress feel warm and unclean and in which he came to a full understanding of the national pleasantry, *Take off your skin and sit in your bones*. On one such day, he was in his bedroom on what the English call the first, and Americans the second, floor. In the last three hours he had taken three cold showers, each of which had given him about five minutes' relief. On this furnace-like summer's day, a breath of air was a vain hope; flowers, bushes, foliage, hung motionless as if painted. An enormous tree in very thick leaf stood close to one of his windows, cutting down by that much the slight hope of a breeze. As he stared resentfully into this dense and shadowed mass, all at once a single branch began to quiver and tremble; something was walking along it, of course, but all the same it looked uncanny, that sudden shivering branch in the deep inert green, moveless as if cast in green lead. As he watched, fascinated, a rat came mincing into view with delicate unhurried steps, and what with its self-satisfied gait and reminiscent smirk, there was no need of the bloody smear on its muzzle to tell what it had been up to. On it came, steadily, straight toward the screened window and quite unaware of the spectator behind it, and with its advance the expression of the triangular face became more and more patent; animals did smile and this thing was smiling; at a distance from Tom of perhaps eighteen inches, it jumped lightly from its bough to a lower one, and was gone. Now, standing in the chill and damp of English November, far removed from that episode but seeing a face momentarily distinct in the pallid street light—especially the lower face—he was forcibly reminded of that other smile, that wicked, three-cornered, rodent smirk . . .

As Michael had diagnosed, this sortie of Ivor's was a trial run. The shock of the encounter night before last, his fright which had magnified the approaching figure to over-life-size dimensions, still revived with uncomfortable vividness whenever he thought of it. Yet for all its recurring quality and lack of subsidence, he had begun to reflect. Was it possible that Auriol was having him followed, and the man had been no more than a private agent tailing him? and in such clumsy fashion, moreover, that the two of them had literally come face to face? Had he *seen* anything of the man, anything—on later consideration—identifiable? The effort, he knew in advance, was vain; the menace walking toward him had been an outline filled in with black, somehow suggestive of shabbiness but with all detail hopelessly submerged . . . With a feral hunger, he longed to know one thing. Was Auriol trying to be clever? If she was, he would make her sorry for an unlimited time to come, and in any number of ways; he was pleasantly aware that the surface of his ingenuity had barely been scratched. The end result of these cogitations was tonight's foray, purely as experiment. If there were the least sign of lurking observation, from whatever distance, he would give up this amusement entirely and devise something else.

The result of the excursion had been entirely gratifying. Not a living creature in evidence, for all his watchfulness and alertness; no one following, on his heels or otherwise. The meeting almost beneath the overhang of the mews archway had been fortuitous, a chance encounter with some denizen of the night up to no good;

some thief or prowler too cowardly to attack him, alone as he was, only as anxious as he to avoid observation.

Emerging from the pub forecourt that held the kiosk, he laughed gently under his breath, standing quite still meanwhile for a final reconnaissance. No one, nobody; wan lamps and empty pavements and streets, emptiness stretching away. Starting down the slight incline, his gait was buoyant and his step elastic. He felt free, triumphant, and scornful of the other night's panic; unpreparedness had done it to him, mere surprise. In his elation he even found a moment of boredom, except that this business was—simply—too excellent a conception to discard, before the last drop had been wrung from it. The shrill summons in his wife's sleeping ear, its association with night, above all with the ominousness and sadness of rain—all this could not fail to make an upsetting picture in her mind, for he knew her as not only imaginative, but highly impressionable . . . Yes, the plan was too good to throw away. Tomorrow night he would pick up the dropped stitch, the night he had missed; artistic integrity was the watchword.

Still, when the door of his safe warm house had shut behind him, he decided otherwise. Three more nights of it, and he was through; actually, he was beginning to find these walks in rain and cold a little strenuous. Yet it was all working out very well, as, for example, the death of the half-witted mother. This had come opportunely, an incontrovertible reason for him to stop the letters, yet under no duress of fear or caution. And in that business of the letters, he was well aware, he had been toying with real danger.

For the rest, he would give himself time to plan the next move for his wife's benefit. And give *her* time to sit, time to wonder what next; time to wait, wait . . .

He would give her, by all means, plenty of time. Perhaps more or perhaps less, according as he found it more or less amusing.

17

His body was Tom M'Kell because it looked like Tom
M'Kell, but only by this resemblance was it his. His
body was empty, except of purpose; his body so subli-
mated to will and intention that it hardly existed, except
as a servant to will and intention. He had heard of this
incorporeal state as a yardstick of the totality of concentration, but he had never experienced it before. An
intermittent murmur brushed the excluding envelope in
which he moved; unaware of hearing or replying, he not
only answered but answered to the point; while wishing
to God it would stop, he hardly identified it as coming
from Michael.

"Get your hand well into the door-grip."

"I know. I've been practising on call-box doors."

"If you fumble it in the least, he's warned."

"I know." *Quit talking*.

"Pull once and pull hard, they're heavy, those
doors."

"I know." *Can't you shut up?*

"Go for his"—Michael was pantomiming to himself
—"his *left* arm, that's it, you pick up with your left and
dial with your right. So go for the left arm, don't let him
ring off at all costs."

"I know." *Christ, shut up will you, shut up!*

"Unless he's left-handed? have you noticed?"

"My God," said Tom, his chrysalis ruptured. "I don't know. He might be."

"In that case, he'd have the phone in his right hand—that much difference might give him his chance to ring off."

"I'll make sure first," Tom muttered. "Thanks for thinking of it."

"Ah." Beside him in the dark, he heard Michael's intake of breath. "Our lad."

Without more speech they followed the familiar tactic, letting the moving dark sliver get well away before they emerged, then watching it till it reached the head of the mews.

"Turning right," Michael murmured, with an undertone of surprise. "Didn't you tell me that's where he got his fright? You'd expect he'd avoid that call-box."

"There're others in that direction." Now at the top of the mews, they watched the swift, barely visible walker. "He's bound for one a couple of streets away."

"Hell," said Michael feelingly, "the further we've got to follow him, the more chance of his seeing us."

"There, he's turning again." Tom's eyes never left the receding figure; again the trance of certainty enclosed him, the poise of the arrow perfectly aimed. "Come on!"

They started a careful jog-trot on the slippery pavements.

"Quick, it's got to be quick." They reached the corner where Hailes had vanished. "He never stops there long. Just two or three rings to wake her up, shove in his threepence, let her listen to nothing, then home again, his good deed well done—There he goes!"

"We should be closer," Michael worried.

"We can't be too close." The slight rasp of tension in his voice was the sole indication that his supporter's anxiety had begun to infect him. "There, he's just going in."

"Well for God's sake, what're we waiting for—"

"Quit crowding me, will you? He's got to dial, she's got to answer, it takes a few—Come on, come on!"

In a frantic burst, half-crouching, they moved.

"Drop behind!" Tom hissed, and the other obeyed.

What followed after that had the blind onrush of nightmare or cataclysm, shattering. Tom, his grip tight in the handhold of the door, tore it open; he flung himself on the slender figure in the box. Even in that fraction of a second, Ivor had time to ring off if instinct had not betrayed him—the compulsive instinct of alarm that made him look around automatically. By that much delay, microscopic, he was lost. One powerful hand gripped and upheld his left wrist; a moment of furious and silent struggle followed. It was in that moment that the other thing happened, the thing unimaginable, unforeseeable, as yet barely flicking Tom's consciousness. His fist was dealing a knowledgeable blow, after which there was no need of his "Drop it!" to make Hailes relinquish the phone; with the nerve-centre in his shoulder clubbed and paralyzed, he had no choice but to drop it. At once Tom retrieved it, saying, "Auriol?" and immediately she answered, "Yes."

"Is anyone there with you?" he demanded, and with like promptness came another voice, "Maggie here—Maggie Bolter."

"Right," he grunted. "We'll be over. One of you be downstairs to open, so we needn't ring."

With one hand still maintaining its crushing hold on the quarry's wrist, and with that other thing still groping in his awareness between light and dark, he wrenched him out of the box. The captive, for all his anomalous position, was obviously readying himself to call for help when he realized the other presence, silent, who had emerged from nowhere, and could be seen to give up the idea. Only his eyes remained alive and calculating, moving from one to the other.

"Now look," said Tom. His voice, hoarse with strain, was low; all around them lay sleeping houses. "We're going to walk to a car. If we meet anyone on the way, a

cop or anyone, and you've got it in mind to shout—
don't." His gaze clamped on the other's gaze as his
fingers clamped on his wrist. "We've witnesses against
you at both ends. We can do this quietly, we'd all prefer
it. Make a row and you'll come out of it badly, I promise you—you're not dealing now with a girl on her own,
or a sick old woman. Will you walk along between us?
not bolt or yell copper or anything?"

Ivor, his face expressionless, nodded,

"Come on then."

"You'll hardly need me, in there?" queried the unknown man—the first word out of him—as they
drew up.

"I expect not," Tom returned. "You'd rather be off?"

"Yes," said the man. He turned his head for a final
stare, long and inscrutable, at Ivor. "See you." As he
moved away, Tom's impaling gaze picked up where the
other's had left off. "Get out," he commanded, "Up
those steps. I'll be behind you."

The street door opened silently before them as they
ascended. Maggie, unkempt in her dressing-gown, pale
and puffy with sleeplessness, closed it behind them and
led the way upstairs. They entered a nondescript living-
room whose lights burned with the tired brightness of
night-watching. Auriol was sitting far to one side as
though seeking the shadow, with a face of blank avoidance; not by a flicker did she signal her awareness that
anyone had entered, and Ivor, with the irrelevant piercing observation of those in dire peril, saw her actual
dread of looking at him. Also he saw in her face the
hunted tensions, the claw-marks of harassment that had
not been there before, and remembering the flawless
cream-and-apricot skin that had been so great a part of
her attraction, thought, *To that extent anyway I've
marked you, you bitch.*

"All right." Tom's voice, recalling him, was not so
much a voice as a succession of hammered spikes.
"Let's not waste time. We've caught you molesting—in-

173

timidating—I don't know what it's called technically, but the police'll know. Now I'm going to dictate a statement that you admit to these calls, also to the anonymous letters to Mrs. Chapman, and you'll sign it. And straightaway thereafter, if you don't agree to whatever divorce arrangements Auriol wants to make, I'll hand over this document where it won't do a practising stockbroker any good. For the present, I'll retain it. When she gets her divorce I'll still keep it, just to make sure there's no resumption of your nocturnal pranks. At the least sign—the very least sign—of that sort of thing starting up again, I take it straight to the police. Now sit down. Here's a pen and paper."

"Everything ready," Ivor murmured. "From your hat. Quite the conjurer."

"Sit down," said Tom. "It's all you've to do, sit down and write. Sit down, I tell you."

"No," said Ivor pleasantly. "I shan't sit down, and I'm not writing anything. You caught me ringing my wife. There's no law against that, is there? and you attacked me in that call-box before I could say a word to her—"

"Say a word," Tom jeered. "You weren't going to say anything, you bastard."

"You can't prove," Ivor returned, imperturbable, "that I wasn't going to speak to her—"

"You were going to wake her up and ring off without speaking," Tom cut him off, "like all those other times before."

"I was going to speak to her." Ivor's murmur was negligent. "You can't prove I wasn't."

"Then why not from your house? why not from your own phone?"

"Because it wasn't working. It's often out of order in wet weather." Out of the corner of his eye he saw Auriol remembering that this was true, and a haggardness come into her face as she saw him getting away; in a lizard-flash he had found the chink of escape in the

174

solid wall. With no trace of his inward smile, he went on, "Ask her if it's not so—ask my wife."

Tom glanced at her; she nodded hopelessly.

"You see." In a dulcet voice, Ivor followed up his victory. "Several times I tried ringing from the house, then I went out to phone—and a couple of cosh-boys jumped on me when I'd just got the number."

"You lying little sod." Constriction of dismay was in his chest, and in his mind a vision—like Auriol's—of a viper slithering free.

"Your word against mine—as they say." Yet with returning confidence all through him, he saw that Auriol avoided looking at him as painstakingly as Maggie; it gave him an unpleasant feeling of having ceased to exist. "Now I'm walking out of here, and I'd like to see you stop me. Raise so much as a finger, and I'll charge you with assault." He regarded the three of them with ascendancy, and with a sort of indulgent amusement. "And I'll press it. I can make a lot of trouble for you, and I'll make as much as possible. I appreciate, of course"—his manner turned silky—"your concern over my wife's divorce. But the lack of it needn't inhibit the two of you, any more than it has done in the past.— Good morning, all!"

"Wait!—Let me talk to him alone." Tom's head jerked a peremptory command at both women; his hard glance never moved away from the figure—lithe, elegant, dressed all in close-fitting black—that had halted involuntarily. As Auriol and Maggie disappeared into the other room, Hailes remained motionless; without concern or alarm and as if barely interested.

"Now look," said Tom. The unacknowledged facet of the call-box incident, swimming nearer and nearer the surface of his consciousness for all his effort to repulse it, held his voice low and gave it a quality almost disembodied, echoing from some unfamiliar cavern of menace. "Either you write that statement and sign it, or I'll say you approached me in the street with indecent proposals, and I'll follow it through all the way. I will, so help me God!"

Whatever breach the threat had made in the enemy's defences, whatever wavering if any, was gone so fast as to make doubtful that it had been there at all; like a cloud-rift it had closed over completely, leaving a front of composure smooth and unbroken.

"I could say as much about you," Hailes returned gently. "When it comes to the point, who assaulted whom? And if your useful friend," he pointed out, a dark gleam of amusement slanting his face like a faun's, "tries to say otherwise, it's perjury. I don't believe he'd oblige you—not to that extent."

"You'll charge *me* with accosting you?" Tom responded at once. "Twist any situation so you'll come out on top, you snake? Damned ingenious." His ironic applause woke a glee in his face that at once echoed, and outdid, Ivor's; ferocious where the other's was merely spiteful, cold and manacing, overlaying the normal texture of flesh with a hard patina of cruelty. "But you've overlooked one thing, perhaps." He paused an instant. "On that point, my life'll bear investigation. Will yours?" He paused again, seeing there was no need to follow up the blow, but following up nevertheless. "I'll lay money that you've been tangled up in something before. And I'll lay money, besides, that the coppers came into it."

At once it was evident: how different everything was between them. A new element had entered into their talk, and the element was fear. The two of them had moved onto ground lethal as a hidden quicksand, whose surface would not bear up a walker's step. He saw it with a newly sharpened, goading vengefulness, and without a trace of pity.

"It's not quite the serious thing it used to be," he pursued ruthlessly. "These aren't the days of Oscar Wilde, I know that. All the same, it's a charge that can still ruin a man. It had ruined them within the last few years, men more important than you—and you won't come off

176

any better than they did. I promise you I'll do you all the damage in my power. I'll destroy you."

Stillness was between them again, a bottomless chasm. Moments passed, too long; just on the point of gesturing toward the table where lay pen and paper, he saw that the other was already moving toward it.

He tapped briefly at the door, opened it a very little, and without looking in said harshly, "It's all right, he won't bother you again. Good night," and escaped rather than left, enveloped—even in the face of having brought it off—by the other preoccupation, complex, that wrapped him like a garment of anger and revulsion and impeded not only thought and reason, but smothered his very breathing.

"I wish you wouldn't go home alone this time of night," said Auriol.

"I'd rather. It's morning anyway, I'll find a taxi. Only—" Maggie hesitated, and the nature of the hesitation, for her, was rare; uncertain, with a visible summoning of her courage "—are you dead for sleep?"

"Am I?" Auriol's glance, half blank, moved here and there without focus. "I shan't know till I go to bed, I expect. Why?"

"If I"—the other's wavering was more marked—"if I could talk to you a moment—"

"What about?"

"Look," Maggie blurted, with an air of taking the plunge, "now that you can go ahead with the divorce—" She stopped abruptly, as if alarmed at her own daring.

"Yes?" asked Auriol. The reference seemed to waken her; her eyes on Maggie were not only concentrated now but aroused, compelling her to finish lamely "—what are you going to do?"

"Sorry." Auriol's moment of alertness passed; she rubbed her forehead. "I don't seem to follow."

"Look," Maggie repeated. "What you've been telling

me about it, while we were waiting here—that you could sue on what amounts to incompatibility, or on the other thing, the nullity—"

"Yes?" Auriol demanded once more. In her whole aspect, again stirred to life, was a covert, suspicious waiting.

"Well, having the choice"—herself not having one, Maggie took the final perilous step—"how are you going to go about it?"

Without the movement of so much as an eyelash, Auriol's stillness of fatigue became another stillness, the coiled immobility before the strike; her face still as death, with far below its surface a smile. The pause that fell between them was as deep and cold as a crevice in ice. At the end of it she said, "I know how I'll go about it."

"Auriol, listen," Maggie besought, "it's not you talking, it's the hatred in you."

"Why not?" said Auriol brightly. "Why not?" All at once her brittle encasement seemed to fall from her in bits. "Maggie," she said abruptly, "thank you for everything, thanks with all my heart, but I must sleep. My head'll fly to pieces if I don't sleep."

"We must talk—"

"Not now, not now, and my God, don't hound me."

"We must"—Maggie strove on in the face of palpable danger—"talk—"

"Later."

"When's later?"

"In a few days maybe, sometime in the next few—"

"That late," Maggie broke in loudly, desperately, "is too late. Well, tomorrow then, promise—promise me."

"All right," Auriol began. "Tomorrow. Or, no," she retracted swiftly, "no, I won't talk about it."

"Auriol," Maggie essayed in final appeal, standing her ground, "Aur—"

"No," Auriol cut her off, in the gentlest voice. Again she was baleful and carven, except that the smile had

178

risen through the marble and faintly moved her lips; motionless she looked straight at her friend, smiling. "Good night, Maggie."

18

His victory over Hailes: blackmail rather, or blackmail
enough to produce a queasiness in him that would not
go away . . . and, with this memory, that other act of the
defeated man, after he had sat submissively writing to
dictation, then signed and stood up to go. Raising his
lids for the first time in minutes, he had given the victor
a long unfathomable glance out of dark, heavily lashed
eyes, a glance with no resentment in it, no hatred, only
—horridly—a mute grief, the sort of reproach that
looks out of a woman's eyes, and his eyes were beautiful
not like a man's but like a woman's, a thing unnoticed
till now. But this reproach that grieved while accepting
—this femininity of reproach—confirmed the whole incident of the call-box. The attack on the figure with the
receiver to its ear; Tom's savage wrenching movement
that brought Hailes around to face him while he tore the
phone from his grasp; the compression of two bodies in
the space that barely took one . . . and then to Ivor's automatic resistance, as savage for a split second as the
onslaught, in the next split second there had succeeded
the other thing, as fleeting as unmistakable; the yielding
of the man pressed against him, a pliancy as in the resistance of love-play, with surrender implicit in its very
resistance. And remembering Ivor's hostility to him on
first sight and the implications of that dislike, its self-be-

trayal measurable in terms of its exaggeration, he grimaced with disgust, feeling tainted; in imagination he flung Hailes on the ground and stamped on him. Simultaneously he shrugged; it was older than Sodom, a thing never totally non-existent among any gathering of males. But his own reaction, disproportionately violent: did this very disproportion and violence conceal, behind repudiation, a perverse attraction? Fling the thought away as he might, it only went to prove the fatal and eternal ascendancy of mindless instinct over anything that man could devise for its control: his poor bridles called education, law, logic, civilizing influences, eternally mended and eternally fraying, the whole futile lot.

"It's not much of a dinner," Auriol apologized in a drifting, lustreless voice.

"That's all right," said Maggie, with token gestures of her fork at the pick-ups on her plate—dry scrambled eggs and mushrooms out of a tin. Before her floated, for an instant, the voluptuous contours of the steak she could have been ingesting either at home or in some good restaurant; her attention claimed by nothing worse than a professional journal or a recent novel, instead of someone else's troubles.

"No, it isn't all right. But I—I felt as if I had to talk, and I couldn't in a restaurant or even your flat or—or anywhere but here. It's like wanting to hide," The words came from Auriol in spurts, jerky, with pauses in between; her voice, its natural quality lost for the moment, had a dry crackling sound like paper. "Or not hide exactly, but just not—not wanting to be seen. When you've been—stripped—in public, you want to crawl into a hole somewhere till you've—got over it. I couldn't have gone out tonight, Maggie, truly I couldn't —yet I couldn't be alone. I couldn't have endured being alone."

"No," said Maggie, and ate some scrambled egg.

"It was awful, awful." Auriol, from a remoteness that took her suddenly and released her suddenly, went on in that dry rushing voice. "You think you're prepared, your barrister has asked you the same questions in private—but when it comes to answering them in public, all alone up there in the witness-box, and the room full of men, nothing but men—"

She broke off again, contemplating some vision of her own; Maggie, stirring her plate with token movements of her fork, glanced at her furtively. Auriol's look, though battered and distraught, was a paradox; her considerable loss of weight gave her the appearance, not of a woman who had been through an ordeal, but of a girl, a slender young girl . . .

"My God, I'm glad it's over. To have that still before me, instead of behind—!" She shivered; yet in spite of shame, revulsion, exhaustion, she must go on spending herself in words, like a hail of dry leaves before a wind.

"Did I tell you, they said my case would be heard *in camera?* they said nullities always were. Well, I took that to mean, literally, judges' chambers, I was all ready for a quaint room with old wainscot and a worn Turkey carpet and légal tomes up the ceiling. Well, it wasn't like that at all. It was just a small courtroom like a shabby sort of schoolroom, and packed, simply packed —and I thought, *Oh my God, must I get up before all of them and talk about . . . they can't be going to do that to me . . . ?* But it was all right," she reassured her past inexperience, with a pallid flickering smile. "All those others were divorce cases too. There must have been a dozen. They were heard first and mine was held to the very last, with my doubtful distinction—of being the only nullity in the lot." Her mouth twisted wryly. "And then the judge simply said, 'The usher will now please clear the court,' and everyone got up and trooped out and then my—my case came on. That's how it was. *In camera* sounds so mysterious, but it only means a lot of empty benches."

Maggie, silent, sat with her eyes as fixed on her scrambled eggs as a diviner's, trying to compel some great truth from their depths. Her lack of comment or reply was beginning to constrain her seriously; moreover, she did not look forward to the moment when Auriol would wake up to it.

"Now I begin to see how fearful it would have been, if Ivor'd defended," she broke out again. "Because of course his counsel would've gone for me with the same vile questions, with lots of insinuation thrown in—" the revulsion that struck through her, stronger than a shudder, stopped her a moment.

"Ivor wasn't there?"

Maggie's neutral voice made it hardly a question, but she was glad to find something to say.

"Not he. And of course that's Tom's doing, somehow. Tom took care of that, however he did it—But I wish you'd seen that courtroom, those other divorce cases." She was whipping the same horse again, full drive. "All there on legal aid, Mr. Dysart said. That mass of inertness without ideas or desire to change, living in the moment for food and cheap amusement. And copulation, so they can produce others exactly like themselves, dull human muck expecting everything to be done for them—and it is. And who pays for it?" With a sudden violent movement she pushed it away. "Let's talk about something else."

The silence after the rush of words had a drained, gutted quality; Maggie broke it finally, asking, "I'll make coffee, shall I?"

"That courtroom." Auriol had not even heard. Despite her interdiction of the subject, apparently she could not keep away from it. "It was wonderful, all the same. That mob, illiterate, you could hardly get anything out of them—a date, a fact, anything. And all of them nervous or frightened, you could tell—a judge who was harsh or sarcastic or impatient, he'd reduce them to mere witless dummies. But that man on the bench, that *angel*." Her eyes and voice were fervent, for an instant, before that vision of humanity. "If you'd seen how he *helped* them—to make a clear story, bit by bit. And with such inexhaustible patience. Oh, he was wonderul. So when I saw how kind he was, I thought it might not be too bad after all. But it was bad enough."

"Yes," said Maggie, or at least intended it so, but it emerged as an undeveloped grunt. "Sit still, why don't you, and I'll clear all this away."

The words—too uncommenting, too inapposite— seemed to awaken Auriol suddenly to Maggie's averted face with its tight, impenetrable look.

"I'm boring you," she said with ominous softness.

Maggie shrugged.

"I'm sorry," Auriol pursued in the same soft voice. "I'm very, very sorry. But I—I thought I was speaking to a friend, you see. I thought a friend might want to know about this frightful thing that's happened to me—"

"Come off it," Maggie interrupted brusquely. To Auriol's startled, unbelieving stare she made no least attempt at concession. "Pack it up."

"Why . . . why . . . "

"My God, I've no patience," Maggie drove on ruthlessly. "All this breast-beating, all these agony calisthenics. You needn't have gone through any of this, you know, if you'd divorced Ivor on the cruelty thing. The only trouble is, that while you wanted to make it hell for him, you didn't bargain for its being hell for you. That part you overlooked or didn't realize or something, and it caught you up. And serve you right—I haven't a vestige of sympathy."

"Why, how *dare*—" The rising outrage in Auriol's voice was defrauded by her shortness of breath. "—how dare—"

"Revenge," Maggie cut in implacably. "It's either vicious or vulgar. The viciousness I can take, but not the vulgarity. You wanted revenge, and I found your way of getting it," she added with explicitness, "thoroughly vulgar."

Inwardly she braced herself to meet whatever she had invoked—reproach, fury, dismissal—and while waiting for it to break on her head, got in a few more words.

"Why, I even tried to head you off from the way you were going, you'll remember, and you weren't having any. So if the whole mess boomeranged on you," she pointed out abrasively, "you mustn't complain. You brought it on yourself—you asked for it."

The silence that fell, imminent with explosion, nevertheless had other and more complex qualities. Auriol, with stiff arms dug in her dressing-gown pockets and a flush in her cheeks, visibly restrained herself from dealing a return blow, and after a moment only remarked, "He wrote letters to my mother." Her voice was emery-dust. "Anonymous letters."

"Nasty," admitted Maggie, suddenly shaken. "Nasty as can be. But you know"—at once she had rallied—"the people that write that sort of muck always turn out to be pitiable, in the end. Miserable creatures with miserable lives, and the misery's gone rotten in them—" She broke off abruptly. "By the way, I didn't know your mother well, but was she affected by those letters?"

"No," said Auriol, after a long, reluctant moment. "Practically not at all. But she might have been," she rallied in turn, contentiously. "No credit to—to *him*—that she wasn't." Any allusion to Ivor, even by pronoun, distorted her mouth slightly. "*He* didn't know but that they might have killed her."

"Yes, well." Both in tone and in manner, Maggie jettisoned the whole apparatus of alleviation—gentleness, consideration, kid-glove handling—in favour of a rising impatience; not only impatience, furthermore, but a rising aggressiveness.

"The intention," Auriol persisted stubbornly. "The intention—"

"We're talking about what happened," Maggie cut her off, "not what might have happened. The intention was inexcusable, I give you that, but your mother wasn't hurt by it, period. Also, little as I knew her," she added with an unbearable air of ascendancy and self-

185

congratulation, "I'd have put money on it that she wouldn't be."

This inflaming smugness produced a sharp movement all through Auriol's body, a spurring of her energies for savage retort. Yet once more, deliberately, she laid a restraint on herself, postponing the moment of satisfaction, of blistering reprisal. Maggie, alive to this nuance of delay, was only half-able to interpret it. She saw it—and felt it—as the finting and shifting of a wrestler, until he could fasten upon his opponent the decisive grip; meanwhile he would hold back, sparing himself, groping and feeling now here, now there, for the final advantage . . .

"Tell me—" said Auriol unexpectedly. A new tautness transformed her all at once, a feral glitter. "Tell me something. That night, when Tom brought—him—here." Again the slight distortion touched her lips, "How did Tom get the upper hand of him, d'you expect? How did he manage it?"

"God, I don't know," Maggie disclaimed. All the fight had gone out of her voice. "I haven't thought of it."

"*I've* thought of it." She looked more intent, more hungry. "I've thought of it, I promise you."

"May I suggest," said Maggie with distaste, "that you could have asked Tom himself, in all this time?"

"I wanted to. I've been going to, again and again." She sat a moment, sombre with the memory of unspoken rebuffs. "And you could see him see it coming, and shying away. He won't talk about it. He doesn't want to and he won't, that's all. But I wonder how he brought him to hell. I wonder, I wonder."

"Just why the hell," Maggie interposed, "are you in such a sweat over it? Why're you so anxious to know?"

"You ask me that? If Ivor Hailes had done to you what he did to me—" Dark triumph was in her face, like a smoky light. "That's why I want to know. Tom didn't catch him out on the letters or the phone calls; he couldn't if those others couldn't. So he did it some other way. But how, how?" A cruel enjoyment lit the triumph. "Oh, I'd *love* to know—!"

Stop gloating, it makes me sick to look at you, was on the tip of Maggie's tongue; just in time she caught it back, sitting during a long pause with a glance of sour avoidance.

"Not all that hard to guess," she said finally. "Obviously he threatened him in some way."

"Of course." In her turn she regarded Maggie with a look of sardonic, unspoken comprehension. "Even I understand that much." Up through her eyes, always more fixed and more menacing, the withheld intention was eating its way out, every moment nearer to surfacing. "Yes, he threatened him. But with what?"

Through the room spread another imminence, of nothing pleasant.

"With blackmail of some sort, I expect," Maggie broke it at last, as if unwilling. "Indecent proposals, something like that."

"Precisely." Auriol snapped the naked bone of contention almost visibly between her teeth; the lier-in-ambush had found the exact moment to pounce. "I married a queer—a homo. And you knew it from the beginning, from that cocktail party of Stormonth's. The moment you set eyes on him," she accused, "you knew it!"

"All right, I knew it," retorted Maggie. "So what?"

"So what! how have you the—the—" Outrage stifled Auriol for a moment. "You could have warned me, couldn't you? But not you, oh no! You knew what I was letting myself in for, you *knew*, and you just let me go ahead."

"Rot! Don't be an ass." A curious duality of tempo seemed to possess Maggie; in her loud quarrelsome voice was a hollowness, in her self-defence an apathy. "Can one adult ever interfere with another, to any effect? If I'd come in with my twopence, would you have done differently? would you have listened?"

"You—you don't know that I wouldn't have listened." The counter-blast had found Auriol unready for only a moment. "You might have made the effort, you might have tried."

"I might have tried and I didn't try because I wasn't inclined to try," said Maggie with brassy explicitness. "You're a big girl, you're in a profession—as I am—that's stiff with queers. If I saw it, why didn't you?"

"I didn't," Auriol rebutted violently. "I just didn't. Up to that time, I'd only had experience with *men*." Her accent was venom. "I took it for granted that if a man pays a woman attention—makes no bones about wanting to marry her, in fact—well then, he's all right. If he isn't, what's he want to go marrying for?"

Her air of unassailable argument came against Maggie's look, deaf and uninterested, and seemed to draw fresh fury and impetus from the sight.

"You won't say? You won't tell me? All right, I'll tell *you*." Her voice became raw with self-pity. "We've all heard of queers who marry for a smoke-screen—to conceal their real inclinations. That's the answer, that's why he married me. Kind of him"—she minced, deadly and silky—"to choose me for the honour. And telling me he wanted children!" A single note of high, glassy merriment broke from her. "I'm glad Tom smeared him underfoot. I'm glad, glad—"

"Shut up," said Maggie. "For Christ's sake, shut up."

"Why? When you might have saved me from all that? You were my friend, you were supposed to be my friend—"

"But not your guardian," Maggie cut in stridently. The air was tainted now with female combat, more raw and more disgusting than any other kind. "Of all the brass, trying to blame me! Am *I* responsible because you're a wide-eyed nit? You lost your right to that ten years ago!"

"Go away," panted Auriol. "Go away, get out of here. A word from you might have saved me, and you couldn't be troubled to say it. Go away."

Maggie, after a moment, rose clumsily. "Auriol," she attempted. "Roly—"

"For God's sake don't, don't—just go. 'Roly!' It's late for that, too late." A lividness transformed her almost beyond recognition. "Go away."

"Yes, yes, I'll go. But just—"

"Get out," said Auriol between her teeth. "Just get out."

"One thing," Maggie strove on against the ejecting violence. With unresistance she resisted, so openly propitiating, so purged of combat, that she looked and sounded humble. "Before you throw me out, just one thing."

During another pause—the vacuum of exhaustion after violence—Auriol's fury dwindled as abruptly as Maggie's, leaving in its wake a smouldering guardedness.

"What?" she demanded sullenly. "What thing?"

"Tell me something," Maggie ventured. With utmost care she readied herself to feel her way, step by step. "You said Ivor'd married you as a sort of camouflage— as a smoke-screen." The allusion made her momentarily hesitant. "You said that."

"I said it," Auriol returned with contempt, "because it's true."

"And what if it's not?" Maggie brought it out almost in a murmur, as if afraid to give it full volume. "What if it's not true?"

"My God." The embers in Auriol's eyes, rekindling, shot sparks of a new incredulity. "Of all the—the—fantastic—Are you taking his part?" she assailed the other suddenly. "My so-charming husband's? He was rotten enough to you, heaven knows."

"Oh, he's got a nasty streak in him," Maggie acknowledged off-hand. "A yard wide, if it comes to that."

"But still you're on his side?" Auriol shrilled. "My God, it's beyond belief. This vile pervert that used me, that simply used me—"

"No." The lethal force of Maggie's voice, cutting her off, was a conviction without passion. "You used him."

The new silence, like a revolving prism, cast on Auriol the varying colours of shock, unbelief, repudiation: finally a rigid hostility, a climactic antagonism.

"If you can explain that," she said at last, "you'd better." Her voice was soft and deliberate. "If you can, you'd better."

"Look," said Maggie, moving onto ground alive with land-mines; her whole aspect advertised that she knew it. "You asked why he married you. He married you because he wanted to. He felt that way about you, to want to marry you. It's simple, it's quite simple. Don't you see?"

"No, I don't see. Did he confide in you?" Auriol's voice and smile, flagrantly insulting, flared all at once to the shape of suspicion. "Unless—unless it's true what I said before, that you knew him. That's it!" she clamoured with sudden denunciation. "That's it! You did know him and you've been lying about it. You knew him and you let me marry him. That's the worst, that's—"

"I wasn't lying," Maggie controverted, roused to trumpeting-point. "I didn't know him from Adam."

"My God, all this *mystery!* if you'd simply explain—"

"I'm trying to explain," the other returned stridently. "If you'd shut up and give me a chance—!" All at once she sagged visibly, as if that final yell had cracked and drained some reservoir of her last energies. "All right, the hell with it," she mumbled. "It's too much anyway, for nearly midnight. Let it go."

"Let it go!" The high-stretched utterance, the hard gleam of her distended eyes, were sparks from her look of malediction. "You think you can say that much, then simply drop it? You'll explain—if you've got to stop here till daybreak—!"

She broke off with a look actually ferocious, and something worse. *Misshapen: stamped with the mis-*

shapen months behind her, thought Maggie all at once, while lamely she offered, "Roly." One person's hatred, more formidable, more frightening than a mob's . . . "Roly, love."

At the endearment—rare with Maggie to the point of non-existence—Auriol's mask broke for a moment with the look of an imminent sob, then hardened again.

"Look." Maggie set herself to plod on patiently. "When you pointed him out to me that first time, it's true, I put him down for a queer. And it did turn me up, the thought of your being involved with him. I didn't know him, I just knew the type—I thought. Well, and then something happened. You were circulating and didn't see it, but I saw it." Her eyes canvassed a long-gone picture. "A man came up and spoke to him. And this man—you couldn't miss it—was pressing him, and Ivor was resisting. He wasn't having any, that's all. And after he'd got rid of the man, his eyes kept following you around the room. He stopped there for quite a while, just watching you. And it was then that I saw I hadn't been exactly right about him."

She paused; Auriol offered no word.

"Real queers, the dyed-in-the-wool ones, they're all right. They're well-off in a way." Maggie's resumption, after moments, had the sound of soliloquy. "They have their society and their friends and their lovers, they have their work and they're clever at it mostly, and they're all right. But the queer that doesn't want to be a queer, that fights his own inmost nature—there's the boy that can be in trouble. Oh, blast, this is difficult—hard work for the late P.M." She scraped the back of her hand across her eyes. "Those men, those half-queers—they can go one way or the other, depending on how circumstances push them, mostly. But here's one man, Ivor, with character and decision, much more than usual with that lot. That's the thing I missed, you see—the thing about him I missed at first. So Ivor's not letting circumstance decide what he'll be or not be. *He'll* have the say about his life, not circumstance. So he's always looking for a girl with whom he can accept the thought of marriage. Or I expect he is. He must, if he doesn't want the alternative."

A gust of weariness blew her voice nearly out; she killed a yawn.

"I don't doubt that he'd had the other thing in his life, often enough. He'd had it, and he wanted to escape it, but he had to have someone who'd help him escape. Not easy to come by, for him. And then he met you, and he thought he'd found it—the escape and the help and whatnot, the—the lifeline he was looking for."

She stopped, visibly letting fatigue swallow her, and sat in a half-doze, looking old, fat, and pale.

"You don't know that," Auriol said after a moment. She looked hollow as a shell, all the fight gone out of her. "You can say it, but you can't know."

"The hell I don't know!" snarled Maggie, stung wide awake by even a dying resistance. "I know because I saw. He met you, and he didn't lose a moment—he grabbed you. And after that I saw you together once or twice. If ever I saw a man court a woman, he was courting you. And you dare tell me I don't know!" Scorn was a lash, almost visible, in her eyes and voice. *"Because he needn't have gone after you like that.* He didn't have to, did he?" She was harsh with demand. "Did he? did he?" Pitiless, she regarded the unanswering figure before her. "Of course he didn't. And he must have been extraordinarily attracted, even to contemplate the idea of marrying—a man like that."

The animus dropped out of her tone; with painful care, she seemed to be feeling her way across some trackless wasteland.

"I don't doubt that he wanted to stay married," she ruminated. "I don't doubt that he wanted a family. And you can't say for sure that it wouldn't have happened, at some time or another. Queers are marvelous fathers, you know. I've seen some semi-tone households like that, and I've never known an exception. Oscar Wilde's youngest son—he never saw his father after he was seven or eight, but he never forgot him. What fun he was, and how he loved the two of them and talked to them as equals, and how they adored him. So I can believe that Ivor hung on as he did, on the chance that things would straighten themselves out. I can believe it without the least difficulty."

A brief silence fell.

"You asked me how I knew," Maggie went on. "Oh, I know, all right. Not just because I saw him with you, either. For another reason."

Her gaze, riveted on distance, painfully sought a path where none was—the path of bitter unwilling self-revelation, vouchsafed before to no living being. "I know because he and I—both of us—are delivered up to misinterpretation by our exteriors. By my looks, I'm papa in a Lesbian combination, aren't I? The pattern, the classic example? Well, actually, I'm mad on men." The brief tearing sound that came from her was a laugh. "When I was young I was desperately romantic, and even now I'm romantic—over men. But supposing I showed it? Look at me!" She laughed again. "With my face, my figure, my voice, I'd make a—a fine show, wouldn't I? So I've a kinship with your Ivor, of sorts. We're both betrayed by our exteriors, I totally, and he —well, at least partly—by the lie that's stamped on our outer casings and always ready to spoil our lives. But he could get away from the calumny of the shell. Or in his case, half-calumny. He was going to get away from that part of himself, or know the reason why." She exhaled forcibly. "Don't you see?"

For another moment she sat frowning slightly before she relinquished the chartless maze she had been exploring; her eyes changed from remote to immediate, her tone from meditative to conversational.

"And those filthy things he did to you after you'd left him—their viciousness was the measure of his disappointment. Of his despair, if you like." She regarded Auriol sardonically. "Or at least, that's how I see it. Not that I claim 20-20 vision, far from it. But I think that's how it was with him. He hoped, poor bastard. He hoped you'd save him from the flaw in himself and make him different. And you were no good to him, as it turned out. You were his bid for a normal life, but somehow you failed him. Why?" Her eyes were pitiless inquiry. "Only you know why. And whether you do or don't, what the hell difference does it make now?" With one elephantine heave, she got out of her chair. "I'm going home."

"I—I—" Auriol, oblivious of the movement of departure, stood aghast, with stricken eyes fixed on things long over; unprepared for the abrupt transference of guilt from Ivor's shoulders to hers, she seemed for an instant to sway beneath the weight of it. "Maggie, it's—it's not so." But her voice, husky and strengthless, implored rather than gainsaid. "I—I was perfectly ready to live with him, it never crossed my mind that we wouldn't. It wasn't my fault, none of it was my—"

"Did you love him?" Maggie asked ruthlessly.

"I—no." She felt naked with culpableness, as when Mr. Dysart had asked the question. "No. But I was affectionate, I—I was willing—"

"Oh, yes." Suave cruelty made Maggie's face a stranger's; for the first time in their long friendship she yielded herself to the unremitting, gnawing thing—her heartsick jealousy of Auriol, a woman able to attract men, and having it in her to attract them for another twenty years. "And most men would settle for affection, wouldn't they? for fondness? But Ivor had to have love," she mocked. "Unreasonable sod. Well!" Enjoying herself, she recapitulated. "Call the whole mess a disparity of expectation. To him, you were everything, a final hope. To you, he was a makeshift—a convenience. He didn't know it, either, so long as you weren't sleeping together. But the moment you were in bed with him, the murder was out. He wanted love, and he found well-bred tolerance. He'd need just a split second to latch onto it, too." She smirked. "If ever I saw intuition on legs, he was it."

"No!" Beset, shaking her head in repudiation, still Auriol strove after her lost vantage-point, her justified grievance. "I *was* willing. I was ready to respond to him and I did, I did—"

"Oh yes," Maggie concurred. "I've no doubt you were . . . conscientious." She closed the hall door behind her on the final word, compelled by mere fallible humanity to implant the poisoned dart, and went downstairs hating herself.

The moment in the call-box lingered with him inexplicably, like a nastiness on one's fingers that would not wash off. But when it lingered on the M'Kell digits for days and days, with unabating unpleasantness, merely to get rid of it he had to confront the image all over again; grope in its unsavoury tangle of roots for the reason why. *Why* had this experience put its mark on him, in this manner? Like the majority of men at some stage of their lives, he had been the object of various advances which he had brushed off without a thought, at worst with annoyance but mostly with amusement. But this tainted feeling, all the worse for being formless, went too deep for brushing off . . .

After long disjointed bouts of reflection, where its elusiveness infuriated him, he was driven to conclude that the answer lay in Hailes himself; in the peculiar quality of the man. His impact of personality, whether for good or evil, was too strong for minimizing or forgetfulness. Seen across a room, he appeared more distinct than other people, hard and distinct as a cameo; Tom remembered this suddenly. So it must be that his power could imprint itself with unusual strength on any contact, brief or sustained, and must be given time to wear away, that was all . . .

And yet, suppose it were not all? suppose he were not to free himself from Ivor Hailes on such easy terms as that? Had he been paltering with the dishonesty that cushions life, when truth is unwelcome or distasteful?

But he had to *know,* unless he knew he could not get free . . .

It was knowledge older than the ages that men and women were dual; he had never thought about it because it could have no application to himself. Now he was forced to think about it. Granted the lurking man in all women, the lurking woman in all men, must there exist corresponding evokers of this duality, from women however feminine, from men however masculine? And in his case that Hailes, much as he loathed him, was for him the arouser of this duality, with its perverted desire? Repugnant as such an answer might be to him, his repugnance was unimportant. But: if in one fleeting moment this single facet of Ivor's could so stamp itself, how must Auriol have fared beneath the stamp of his other facets, die-cut with the same cruel power? How vulnerable she would have been, poor unsuspecting creature, how defenceless before such razor-edged attack. Her altered face rose before him, her ill-used beauty. Painful, it was all too painful, he must think quickly of something pleasant . . .

The rub was that there was nothing pleasant to think of. Hastily he brought Christine before him; the thought of getting in touch with her again, of patching things up after their quarrels, had always been a source of delicious torment and excitement . . . Yet now he frowned, a frown with a groping quality in it, like a blind man whose stick fails to encounter a reliable guide-post. There was no power in the thought of Christine, the virtue had gone out of it. Through his comfortless sense of bankruptcy, he wondered why. The alchemy of events, changing him from what he had been? preoccupation with one person somehow dimming another? For the face that was present to his mind's eye was not Christine's, nor was it beautiful at the moment; it was less attractive than he had ever known it. How pleasant it would be to see it regain its former felicities of charm and spirit, he thought with a protective benevolence, then—all at once—with something that had nothing to do with benevolence, something sharp and deep and intense, like pain . . .

In mind and in body he halted, brought up short by a new astonishment. Why, at his very hand there might be a door opening on a room, a room long unperceived but full of light and warmth, of lovely excitement . . . and even at the thought of trying the door, even with no assurance that it would open for him, his breath failed suddenly and his knees went weak.

19

She had pushed all the irrelevant things away from her; the insignificant things like her nervousness and shrinking, her agonized reluctance. All this could make no difference to what she had to do, and which there was no escape from doing.

Shuttered against weakness and cowardice and most of all against thought, her passage down the mews had the dimly lit, imprisoning quality of a dream that goes on forever. Around her automaton's feet, pale gleams were blown alight and blown out, random alms of a full moon behind a tattered overcast; this too was shut away from her mind no less than the coming interview, on whose nature she would not even speculate, and on whose inexorable necessity impringed only one question: would he be there? would he be at home? For if he were not, she doubted that she would have the courage to try again. Her present attempt was quite unannounced, since the thought of ringing him induced a revulsion all through her . . . The house confronted her, shrouded as usual against any informing ray of light; she rang the bell and waited, then heard slight sounds of approach and hoped with a cowardly hope that it would be one of the Patchams that answered.

The door came open silently and it was Ivor; the light was so bad that his face was unreadable. He made no sign of recognition, surprise or anything other, but simply stood there. His utter stillness, together with her own uncertainty, deepened the abyss between them till mere devastation had forced from her a wavering "May I come in? a moment—?" To this he responded with a further immobility, then with a vague motion, debatably permissive, and so very slight that on entering she had to brush uncomfortably close past that figure as dark, and as secret, as carved basalt. As she passed along the hall she was thinking that ordinarily she would expect him to be out, that his ever-ready scorn of people did not preclude him from hating to be alone; obviously events of the last months—and one final event—had driven him deep into an unnatural solitude, and she felt a stab of forlorn and unavailing compunction.

In the living-room he still offered no word or invitation to sit down, nor did she wait for it, facing him at once. By the brighter illumination his face was expressionless and his eyes large but blank, two holes cut out of an inner darkness. To this mask, trying not to let it unnerve her, she offered what she had to say, because she had no choice.

"Ivor, I'm sorry about all this, I'm sorry, I'm sorry" —she began talking fast—"and I wanted to tell you that all the blame—it's mine, all of it, all of it's my fault. I should never have married you, I did it for the wrong reasons and all of it—all of it afterward—came from that. It was all my fault."

She drew a breath, audible and ragged, not helped in her difficult task by any response on his part; no acceptance, no rejection, nothing but that blank look fixed on her steadily.

"If I'd loved you," she pursued infelicitously, "if I'd really wanted you, if I'd been ardent, things would have been all right between us. I see that now, I didn't before."

Hard, increasingly hard to labour on against that impenetrable silence, those eyes lightless as the void. Nevertheless—

"It was I that made the whole thing . . . nothing," she strove. "I had nothing to offer you, I was dead and empty and I married you for something to get hold of, anything—I did it for myself, only for—I did that terrible thing to you, wicked, it was wicked—"

Now beyond her realization of her useless errand and beyond her plummeting sense of failure, loomed another thing: the peculiar emanation of the presence standing before her. This quality, not less alarming for being indefinable, stirred her to a first sudden panic and awareness of her folly—of having walked into a house to be alone with it. And the flare of terror in her, instantly controlled if not quelled, was patent to him, he quickened slightly to her smell of fear like an animal, and the movement was as imminent with danger as an animal's crouch. All at once she wanted madly to flee, to whirl and go tearing out of the room, out of the house, out . . .

"Forgive me," she managed all the same, the withheld fear shaking her voice, and forced herself to look full at him. "I don't mean now, but sometime when you've put me where I belong—in the discard—among your mistakes. Because you—you found me out from the first. You knew, didn't you?" she propitiated hopelessly. "I wouldn't inflict that on anyone alive—that loneliness—"

On a gasp she fell silent, for he was smiling; it shocked her, like an electric current.

"Loneliness?" he murmured, the first word out of him since she had entered. "On the contrary. Who's lonely with three in a bed? you and I and—Giles?"

The rawness even of this taunt came home to her incompletely, already encased as she was by necessity—dreaded, inexorable—to say the thing that was unsayable, to repair with useless words the irreparable.

"And with all my heart—Ivor—"

How was it, protested an invincible part of her, that terrible things always carried in themselves the weakness and taint of melodrama?

"—I beg you to forgive me for the divorce, for suing you on—those—grounds—"

Now she had said it and could hear again her clamour of instinct to escape, but she stood paralyzed; mired knee-deep in her sense of mounting danger but not knowing how to end it; words abysmally inept kept coming out of her, words and words.

"—for I needn't have done it—like that. I needn't have done that to you. Ivor, please—"

The basaltic figure cracked from its immobility, lifting an arm and striking her hard across the face. The lightning movement was such that her surprise offset the pain; astonishment, for the moment, was a sort of anaesthesia. After the brief pause of stupefaction, and dimly aware that his expression had not changed at all, she turned and made her way a little unsteadily down the hall. No footfall came after her on the thick carpet, no one was behind her as she let herself out.

The same trance of incredulity served her well, preserving her immune to thought and feeling as she emerged from the mews and walked another long block. Only then did she wake to the fact that her upper lip and front teeth hurt considerably, and for the first time she began to put her hand to her face and wonder what sort of figure she would cut in tomorrow's daylight. With no handbag on her and no mirror, she began seeking her reflection in any polished surface. Here was something—a display of shoes brilliantly illumined and mounted on columns of mirror. She looked furtively along the street, left and right, then bent forward . . . astonished, then relieved, she saw nothing but a little redness under her nostrils and a slight blurring of the contours of her mouth. The inside of her upper lip was torn where the blow had driven it against her teeth, but apart from that nothing that could not be dissimulated by make-up for a day to two; nothing at all.

There's no mark on me, she thought, then heard incongruous echoes of the child's game: *Never touched me! Never touched me!* But the echo in her was only of wonderment, not triumph; there was no triumph in her, only incredulity that the dismissive powers of the mind were so boundless, that violence must carry in itself its own oblivion, the need to bury the ugly thing, forget it. And she was unresentful, perfectly unresentful. The vicious blow, far from reviving any sense of injury against her husband, evoked from her only a strange compliance. It was his final protest against the cheat she had practised on him and the injury she had done him. Yes, the hard stroke across the face was her desert. And not only her desert, but somehow his right.

She was walking now beside a long dark stretch of square garden; through its mesh fence straggles of privet hedge, ill-kempt, and in her nostrils was the smell of earth-mould and matted leaves and the faint bitter tang of grimed foliage. For comfort against this seasonal death and against the vast and disowning night, she evoked her refuge, the thought of Giles, three years dead . . . all at once she had halted, a faint unconscious perplexity between her brows. When she began moving again, her slower gait reflected the perplexity of her face. It was not only that Giles had failed to come with accustomed vividness, but—she recognized—that her call for his presence had been less urgent. At once she tried to repudiate the implied faithlessness of this, but all that would come was the illogic—overwhelming— of: *I'm alive, I'm glad I'm alive,* that suddenly shaped itself into another phrase, unbidden: *time to say good-bye.* And beneath her shame, and the old habit of grief that smote her like the backwash of a wave, this time she did not go down, drowning, but fought to remain on the surface.

My love, she entreated Giles, always moving along the tree-dark enclosure, *if you'd lost me, you'd have had to get over it, I'd have wanted you to get over it. I loved you, and I wanted to die. But now I don't want to die, I want to go on living as long as I can.* A mere formless excitement of life rose in her, disturbing and inchoate, an eagerness still uninhabited by any living image. Pleasure in drawing breath, in feeling how easily she walked was, for the moment, enough.

Now she rested in a contentment strange to her; it was long since she had felt contentment. The old grief might return to flaw it, but always now with lessened force against a new grief of knowledge: that the living being, possessed by the dead, is a carrier of lethal injury. Injury such as she had done Ivor when she went to bed with him clad in the mournful cerements of second-best; the injury of offering to his razor intuitions her joyless lovemaking, trammelled by her regret and submission to her hard luck; incalculable injury, the withered harvest of having lived in bond to the dead. But now she was ready to dispute her bondage; she would not live blasted and frozen as she had done, and touch others with the ice-cold hand of her servitude to death . . .

Walking always, she fixed her eyes unseeingly on the bare branches of a tree still distant. Behind it were the broken sky and the gleams that haunted it, the struggling moon distinct then obscured, like a swimmer in heavy surf. Now a wider field of cloud, snow-flocculent, turned suddenly to silver, and against this moony dapple the winter tree stood all at once as if clothed in white blossom. In the next instant the light was withdrawn, the tree was barren again—a winter tree against a winter sky. But it made no difference. The moment of transfiguration, of fleeting, piercing beauty, had been enough . . .

Enough, came to her unpremediated, *it's enough, enough.* She was not sad or submissive, only reasonable, consenting to the unreason of life. Such consent could not have been possible to the girl who loved Giles, but she was not the same girl, time and events had made her different. Only the dead remained unchanged, not the living.

I loved you, she consoled Giles. No: Giles had never needed consolation.

But what I was, she told him, *will always be faithful to what you were.*

And having let him go, yet keeping him forever, she had no timepiece to mark the precise moment when she had been healed of despair.

BELMONT NOVELS OF LOVE & ADVENTURE

BELMONT GOTHICS OF EXCEPTIONAL INTEREST

THE TUNNEL (B60-2025) by Anthony Bristowe   60¢
Young Annora Sullivan finds malice and menace at Merton Manor.

THE HOUSE ON SKY HIGH ROAD (B75-1096) by Isabel
    Stewart Way   75¢
A young girl is employed at a mysterious house in the California
wilderness.

THE DARK WATCH (B75-2007) by Genevieve St. John   75¢
A young girl in rural New York meets a strange, fierce man in a
lonely, old house.

THE VICTORIAN CROWN (B75-2042) by Edwina Noone   75¢
Dark forces in her own home threatened her happiness, her romance,
even her life.

HOUSE OF DEADLY NIGHT (B75-2060) by Iris Barry   75¢
Lucinda, a young nurse, goes to an estate in Oregon to tend a handsome patient surrounded by murder.

ANNIE (B95-2070) by Gloria Jahoda   95¢
A touching novel of an orphan maid whose love is strong enough to
survive two marriages.

DESTINY'S CHILD (B75-2071) by Patricia Morton   75¢
When she loses her fiance and her brother, young Julie travels to
France where she uncovers a ghastly secret.

SECRET OF THE WILLOWS (B75-2077) by Elna Stone   75¢
A girl travels to a Southern plantation to visit her sister's grave and
meets the ghost of a Civil War belle.

THE SECRET OF DRESDEN FARM (B75-2088) by Genevieve
    St. John   75¢
Spell-binder about a young girl's attempt to claim her legal inheritance.

DEATH HALL (B75-2089) by Mary Reisner   75¢
Horror-ridden tale of a young girl's struggle to stay alive and keep
faith with her husband accused of murder.

THE LONG AND LIVING SHADOW (B75-2098) by Daoma
    Winston   75¢
Mickey had to offer herself as bait to find out who wanted to kill
her and claim Bassett Place.

Belmont Productions, Inc., 185 Madison Avenue
New York, New York 10016

Please send me the books listed below.

ORDER BY BOOK NUMBER ONLY.

Quantity	Book No.	Price
. . . .	. . . .	. . . .
. . . .	. . . .	. . . .
. . . .	. . . .	. . . .
. . . .	. . . .	. . . .
. . . .	. . . .	. . . .
. . . .	. . . .	. . . .
. . . .	. . . .	. . . .

In the event we are out of stock of any of the books listed, please list alternate selections below.

. . . .	. . . .	. . . .
. . . .	. . . .	. . . .
. . . .	. . . .	. . . .
. . . .	. . . .	. . . .

I enclose $. . . . .

NAME . . . .

(please print)

ADDRESS . . . .

CITY. . . . . STATE. . . . . ZIP. . . . .

Send cash, check or money order. Add 15¢ for every Canadian dollar order. Please allow 4 weeks for delivery. Please add 15¢ per copy for mailing.